CW01239342

LIVES OF BITTER RAIN

ALSO BY ADRIAN TCHAIKOVSKY

THE TYRANT PHILOSOPHERS
City of Last Chances
House of Open Wounds
Lives of Bitter Rain
Days of Shattered Faith

SHADOWS OF THE APT
Empire in Black and Gold
Dragonfly Falling
Blood of the Mantis
Salute the Dark
The Scarab Path
The Sea Watch
Heirs of the Blade
The Air War
War Master's Gate
Seal of the Worm

TALES OF THE APT
Spoils of War
A Time for Grief
For Love of Distant Shores
The Scent of Tears (with Frances Hardinge et al.)

ECHOES OF THE FALL
The Tiger and the Wolf
The Bear and the Serpent
The Hyena and the Hawk

CHILDREN OF TIME
Children of Time
Children of Ruin
Children of Memory

DOGS OF WAR
Dogs of War
Bear Head
Bee Speaker

FINAL ARCHITECTURE
Shards of Earth
Eyes of the Void
Lords of Uncreation

OTHER FICTION
Cage of Souls
Alien Clay
Service Model
Guns of the Dawn
Spiderlight
Ironclads
Firewalkers
Ogres
Walking to Aldebaran
One Day All This Will Be Yours
And Put Away Childish Things
Saturation Point
The Doors of Eden
Feast and Famine (collection)

LIVES OF BITTER RAIN

ADRIAN TCHAIKOVSKY

HEAD
of
ZEUS

An Ad Astra Book

First published in the UK in 2025 by Head of Zeus Ltd,
part of Bloomsbury Publishing Plc

Copyright © Adrian Czajkowski, 2025

The moral right of Adrian Czajkowski to be identified as the author
of this work has been asserted in accordance with the Copyright,
Designs and Patents Act of 1988.

All rights reserved. No part of this publication may be: i) reproduced or transmitted in any form, electronic or mechanical, including photocopying, recording or by means of any information storage or retrieval system without prior permission in writing from the publishers; or ii) used or reproduced in any way for the training, development or operation of artificial intelligence (AI) technologies, including generative AI technologies. The rights holders expressly reserve this publication from the text and data mining exception as per Article 4(3) of the Digital Single Market Directive (EU) 2019/790.

This is a work of fiction. All characters, organizations, and events portrayed
in this novel are either products of the author's imagination or are used fictitiously.

9 7 5 3 1 2 4 6 8

A catalogue record for this book is available from the British Library.

ISBN (HB): 9781035911448; ISBN (GOLDSBORO HB): 9781035924165
ISBN (EBOOK): 9781035911455

Map © Joe Wilson
Typeset by DivAddict Solutions

Printed and bound in Great Britain by
CPI Group (UK) Ltd, Croydon CR0 4YY

MIX
Paper | Supporting
responsible forestry
FSC
www.fsc.org   FSC® C013604

Bloomsbury Publishing Plc
50 Bedford Square, London, WC1B 3DP, UK
Bloomsbury Publishing Ireland Limited,
29 Earlsfort Terrace, Dublin 2, D02 AY28, Ireland

HEAD OF ZEUS LTD
5–8 Hardwick Street
London EC1R 4RG

To find out more about our authors and books
visit www.headofzeus.com
For product safety related questions contact productsafety@bloomsbury.com

*To Shane, Wayne and Martin,
companions from my own early years.*

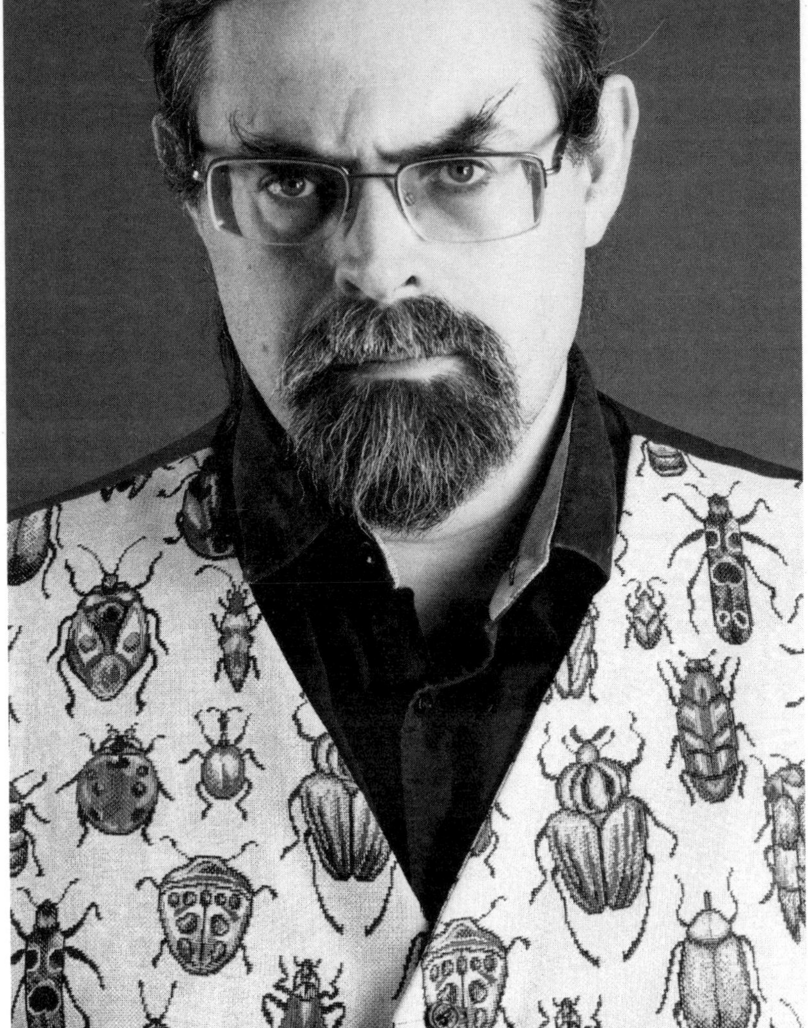

About the Author

ADRIAN TCHAIKOVSKY is a British science fiction and fantasy writer known for a wide variety of work including the Children of Time, Final Architecture, Dogs of War, Tyrant Philosophers and Shadows of the Apt series, as well as standalone books such as *Elder Race, Doors of Eden, Spiderlight* and many others. *Children of Time* and its series has won the Arthur C. Clarke and BSFA awards, and his other works have won the British Fantasy, British Science Fiction and Sidewise Awards.

The Palleseen Sway

- Telmark
- Bracinta
- Jarokir
- Oloumann

Oloumann · Sansovaal · The Miseries · Stouk · Teeth of Reason · Holveillor · Allor · Jarokir · Killinbraan · Pallesand · Bracinta (Magnalei) · Loruthi Palatinate Territories

Map

Farasland
Gallieta
Ilmar
Jelmark
Divine City
Vhishtinlant
Tecuvir
Lor
Austegrande

Austentarn
Eres Ffenegh
Eres Alvegh
Elder Skoam
Successor Steppes
Goshumaj
Peor
Usmai
Alkhalend
Lucibi
Lemas
Usterlant
Haesserlant
Cotto
Bridge
Scorsvent
Fungan Maeren
Khoal
Laneph

Scale

★ ★ ★

Eres Ffenegh

Usmai

Successor Steppes

Allor

A Fire out of Season

The bell tolls, but the rains mutes it to almost nothing. It's made from one of the old temple constructs, that had been battering the liberating forces just a couple of years ago. Now there's only a hollow, rounded torso suspended on ropes, struck on the hour – the Palleseen hour – by a hammer connected to a water clock. And the water from the rains gets into the clock, despite everyone's best efforts, meaning that in the two months of Jarokir's deluge season the bell strikes at all times and the garrison's learned to ignore it. If they even register it over the constant drumming of the weather.

Angilly is twelve, a child of soldiers. Her father is a statlos attached to the garrison's quartermaster office. Her mother is a Fellow-Inquirer from Correct Speech. When she was three years younger, and before she came with her family over to Jarokir, she thought that meant that it was her mother's job to know everything. Now she's twelve and here, she thinks it's her mother's job to ask all the awkward questions which, when you're twelve and just starting to evaluate who you are and where you fit in the world, is the worst thing. This shift in perception has nothing to do with travelling across the sea to Jarokir and everything to do with growing up.

In fact, her mother's role as an Inquirer is to interrogate Pals and their Accessories for potential disloyalty, and put the screws on local Jarokiri suspected of harbouring religious views and/or people, both of which are expressly banned under the perfection that the Palleseen have brought to Jarokir. Angilly will only understand this a lot later, and wonder what she would have thought, had she understood it when she was twelve. Because, make no mistake, her petty rebellions against her mother's rule – her father being only a mute and yielding Accessory to maternal authority – do not extend to questioning perfection. Back on the Archipelago she had sat in Junior phal and learned by rote all the essential truths that explained why the Palleseen way was best, why the Palleseen Sway was necessary and the terrible, degrading conditions that people lived in, who hadn't been brought into it. And now she's here in Jarokir where people really do seem to live in terrible, degrading conditions, and every day she sees her people try to help them by explaining how to live by the precepts of Palleseen ordnances. She's watched this for years, in the heat, rain and dry, and somehow the locals never get any better off, and many of them seem just to become poorer and meaner, and obviously that's their fault. She believes, like most Pals believe, that the Jarokiri are just innately less perfect, but surely they can learn, if they only let go of their superstitions and nonsense, and just *try*.

She wasn't there for the liberation of course. What the Jarokiri are still mostly calling the invasion, because they aren't perfect yet. She didn't see the wonder of the temples, the resplendent cities, the craftsmanship, the artifice. Not that it has been erased, of course, but repurposed. The divine script and holy symbols scrubbed off or defaced or repainted. So that those examples of Jarokiri high culture she has seen register as Pal to her, based on whose livery they sport and whose hands they are in.

And Jarokir isn't the Archipelago. She has fewer and worse friends, and the circle of people her mother feels like associating with is cripplingly small, and the little phalanstery here is undersupplied with books and the teacher is just a Cohort-Archivist with two other full-time jobs to do as well. And inwardly she shifts the blame for all these inconveniences onto the Jarokiri for not allowing themselves to be perfected quickly enough.

Today she will see another side of the Jarokiri.

The bell tolls and tolls again, and nobody hears or cares in the garrison refectory. Angilly and her class are having their lunch here. They eat the rolled bread ammies like soldiers do, because if it's good enough for the marching feet of the Palleseen army then it's good enough for kids. She sits in the middle of a row and tries not to knock elbows with her neighbours. You grow up en masse, as a Pal kid, even a Fellow-Inquirer's girl. She's been in the company of various peers all her life. You learn to do a lot of things in close quarters, including bathe and eat. There's a whole passive-aggressive etiquette about what you do with your elbows, that can go anywhere from flirting to bullying.

She keeps her elbows to herself. A week before – a Palleseen week – she put one of those elbows in the ear of a boy who had been constantly jamming his into her arm, and that had seen her up before the teacher. Who hadn't known what to do with her because her mother was the Fellow-Inquirer. And anyway, her mother had been far worse and more severe.

A boy on the far side of the table – not elbow-jabber – says, "Anyone else smell smoke?"

Nobody else smells smoke. And the walls are creeping with damp, and so what, honestly, would the odds be?

Everyone's been complaining for a month about trying to get fires to even light.

Except there is smoke. Angilly lifts her head, frowning. When she concentrates, when she's thinking hard, her face screws up like a wizened apple, like a hundred years of puzzled sagacity drop over her features. Her mother is constantly telling her that she looks like one of those undead monkeys the local temple used to have, before the liberators threw them on a fire in the name of decency.

Under the dripping ceiling, dark curls coil like hair.

Around that time, the boy across from her spits out his mouthful. "This tastes rotten," he says. He has no manners, and everyone ignores him for the half-second it takes for them to find that their own ammies have gone abruptly rancid. Angilly peers into hers and sees things crawling there, seething out of the blackening bread and greenish meat.

The officers – her mother included – are dining at the top table. Now one of them stands up, flipping his own plate, looking greenish.

"It's an attack!" he bellows. "It's a curse attack! Everyone out and someone check the countermeasures!"

Teacher crosses to the door and opens it unwisely. Unwisely because he should have noticed the heat through the handle. The inferno that ravens hungrily into the refectory catches his uniform shirt on fire almost instantly and he staggers back, screaming.

Angilly, her mouldering ammie still in her hands, stares blankly.

The fire rushes into the room. It isn't acting like fire. It seems to have a serpent's body, a lizard's legs. It seizes the nearest table in its jaws and abruptly the wood – the dank, saturated rainy-season wood – is ablaze. The refectory only has the one door.

Abruptly the air in the room is choking. Not just the smoke, which is descending on them all like a flight of smothering black-winged birds, but some innate foulness rising from the spoiled food. Some of the rank and file soldiers are running for the door, then falling back from the eager flames. Others clutch for their batons, as though this is a foe they can shoot. Angilly can hear the bell now, faintly through the high, narrow, defensible windows. Too high, narrow and defensible to get out through.

Some of the children are crying or screaming now, but Angilly is twelve, and so she's far too old for that. She just stands there, face screwed up, trying to think what to do.

The fire is virtually in her face when strong hands grab her by the ribs and pick her up. She will, forever, have a tiny shiny mark on her chin, from where the searing serpent flicked its tongue at her. Then her father has her. Her mother is busy shouting orders that will not, in the end, accomplish anything. Her father has her under the arms, though. He, the solid statlos, the clerk, muscles her to one wall, clambers up on a table that is already smouldering. He thrusts her at the window.

It is too small. If she was five. If she was eight, even. But she's twelve. She's too big and grown up to fit through windows like some child.

Her father, who has only ever been an echo of her mother's harsh voice all her life, has found his voice now. He lays down a parental line, an unyielding rule of conduct for his solitary daughter. *You will go through this window.* He takes no lip from her. Even when she kicks him in the face he won't desist. As though this is some iron precept of perfection they somehow omitted from the curriculum at the phal.

He gets her head into the gap. Her shoulders wedge. She twists, getting them into the diagonal, crying, screaming at him that he's hurting her. Her father, the monster, the brute.

He shoves. Beneath his feet, the table grinds across the stone floor. The stone floor that is smouldering, the very damp of it catching like oil. The table that is leaping with flames that nip at his shins and ankles. He shoves until her shoulder dislocates. He rams at her until her head snaps the latch of the shutters and the rain and sun and firelight is in her eyes, and splinters across her face. He forces her through the bottleneck of the window and doesn't stop when her forearm, twisted awkwardly across her body, snaps, one bone then the other. He doesn't stop until enough of her is in the torrential outside that momentum and gravity carry her through and she's gone.

Then he turns and grabs the next nearest child and does it again, but Angilly only picks that up in retrospect. Afterwards, when she's in the infirmary with the others, the coughers, the burnt, the sick.

Lying in the mud beside the garrison wall, Angilly sees them. The enemy. They run through the compound with torches that only burn brighter for the rain. With knives, that they try to get into any Pal they can find. They spin and collapse sometimes, when a soldier can bring his baton to bear.

One of them is on fire. Not on fire like her father is on fire. Like her mother and the others trapped in the refectory. On fire like robes. Striding through the mud and leaving blackened, hissing footprints. A woman with a face like the sun. A priestess, Angilly understands. One of the monsters that Jarokir was liberated from. A sacrificer of children, a slave to monstrous divinities. She gestures, and things that shouldn't even burn spring alight and crackle. Stone cracks, the rain flashes into incendiary sparks.

In the garrison, her parents and most of her classmates burn.

Merely Adequate

She would see Jarokir again, but not for many years. After the infirmary came the ship. She and a handful of others, children, the badly injured, a few old-timers grabbing for early retirement. Heading back to the Archipelago. As though fate had heard her ardent pleas about not being sent away to some foreign land, and granted her wish in its own time, and in the worst way.

On the Archipelago it was the orphanage for her. Thorntree House, they called it. Perhaps unfair to say it was as bleak as that sounded. The Pals were good with orphanages. Not that they weren't strict, always ready with the switch for discipline and a variety of other punishments. But then Pal adult life was hardly short of discipline or punishment, as any soldier who'd gone to make an account for the Tally officer would tell you. The Pals believed in preparing children for the way things would be. But that same doctrine provided a prescribed but practical educational discipline. Philosophy, history, science, mathematics, all the pillars that held up perfection. Approved literature, from the limited canon of perfection. A set of skills befitting an officer's career in army or administration. And some students went further and learned specialities. The disciplines resulting from the Pals taking skills and crafts and magical traditions from the people they were perfecting, filing away all the ritual and nonsense and leaving people with something baggage-free and useful.

Angilly has no particular aptitude for any of those novel and slightly unsound-feeling disciplines. She has performed passably in all the standard areas. Her particular specialities are not useful from the perspective of a career. She is active, quick on her feet. She always comes near the front when there's a race – long or short – or an obstacle course. She picks up outdoorsy skills swiftly. When one teacher started a fencing ring amongst the students, she became the unquestioned queen of the star-shaped piste. Thrashed every opponent with, perhaps, an undue degree of enthusiasm. Easy to read it as exorcising trauma for the deaths of her parents, but it's an orphanage for a state whose chief export is violent conquest, and so Angilly's story is hardly unique.

Fencing is a garnish, on the skillset of a career officer. Not something that will, in itself, lead to preferment. And Angilly doesn't necessarily want preferment. At fifteen, she doesn't really know what she wants, except that she's not keen on maths. But she's a year off being assigned to one of the Schools, and she's not good enough at anything to find a decent position, even if she's not so dull that she'll just get kicked down into the ranks. She'll just drift, end up some clerk's assistant, a quartermaster, a watch officer. Some menial but useful cog in the Palleseen machine.

Good enough for her. But not, as it turns out, for Aunt Ostrephy.

Angilly is vaguely aware that she has an Aunt Ostrephy. She met the woman a couple of times when she was much smaller, before going away to Jarokir, her memory preserving only the general sense of a kind of personified disapproval.

Disapproval that her mother, Ostrephy's sister, had married a mere statlos, if nothing else. Disapproval that Angilly herself wasn't a perfectly-behaved six-year-old capable of reciting the Precepts without hesitation or missing words.

After the incident, the woman's name had been vaguely in the air concerning Angilly being accepted into Thorntree House, because it was relatively exclusive as orphanages went. The children there were all of a certain standing or family. Everyone had an Aunt Ostrephy-equivalent to vouch for them, or else their parents were just overseas and they had become orphans-of-convenience like so many on the Archipelago. Not everybody took their children when they received an assignment that required travel.

Angilly has been fighting again. Meaning – unlike when she was younger – actually formally duelling with blunted foils, in a socially-acceptable manner. She won. She always wins, and isn't quite sure why. The teacher who set up the circle talks a lot about the drive to dominate and succeed, but that isn't how she feels about it. She mostly just really enjoys it, the elegance, the footwork, the angles. Fencing speaks to her about both perfection and mathematics in a way that her regular lessons do not. And right now fencing is definitely an encouraged pastime for an officer. The stern eye of perfection won't start to frown at the tradition for at least another decade or so.

Aunt Ostrephy is a woman ahead of her time, in that. She doesn't seem to much approve. When Angilly arrives for their meeting in a grimy shirt, breeches unbuttoned at the knee, still towelling the sweat from her hair, the old woman doesn't appreciate it. For Angilly's part, she hadn't realised she was having a meeting with her Aunt Ostrephy, as nobody had told her. The woman is just sitting in the common room, and nobody else is. Two whole years of the better class of orphan just banished, because Aunt Ostrephy wanted to set an ambush.

"Sit," she tells Angilly. The woman has taken the short end of one of the long study tables, meaning that either Angilly sits so far from her that she would have to strain to hear, or she takes a pointedly subordinate position. Which she does, as sulkily as only a fifteen-year-old can.

"I am," says Aunt Ostrephy, "your aunt," which finally allows Angilly to place her, because honestly she'd just seen a heavyset axe-faced old woman with a Fellow's insignia on her uniform jacket. Old, in this case, meaning thirty-nine years, which judgment a thirty-nine-year-old Angilly will later look back on and roll her eyes at her younger self.

When she's seated, and when the icepick stare of her aunt makes it plain just who is talking right now and who is listening, Ostrephy says, "I have left matters this long in case you were simply dealing with the grief." A stress on that last word, suggesting that grief is one of the long list of things that perfection will eventually get around to eradicating from the world. "Pray tell me, what is this?"

A piece of paper, a familiar one. A report card. Angilly's competences. A jab of the older woman's blunt finger. "This word, are you capable of reading it?"

The teacher's handwriting is entirely clear. "Adequate," says Angilly, and then her ear is ringing and the world spins a bit because Aunt Ostrephy has clipped her about the side of the head, swift as a striking snake.

She knows that precise grade of disapproval from the stricter teachers. She hadn't realised it came in Aunt-sized slices too. "Magister," Angilly adds, because Ostrephy is an aunt, but she is also a *Fellow*, which is a fine rank to have, higher than many attain.

"Adequate," Aunt Ostrephy says, "is not acceptable. Not for my niece. Not for Ariet's only daughter. Ariet was never *adequate*. I was never *adequate*. Our family does not tolerate *adequacy*."

Angilly isn't entirely sure *adequacy* is a word, but argument is plainly contraindicated by the prevailing balance of power. She just stares mulishly.

"I have spoken to the staff here," Ostrephy says. "They inform me that you are currently on the very margin of passing your officer's credentials. A grade that might see you as some broker's storehouse clerk or a menial officer at the foot of a company rank ladder, never to climb much higher. Very *adequate* positions."

There are the usual aphorisms about all these roles contributing to a greater perfection, and there is Angilly's personal take which is that she doesn't actually care about any of it and any role is as bad as any other. Neither of which would, she divines, meet a receptive ear at this moment.

"Do you see this? Can you tell me what this means?" Aunt Ostrephy displays the full shoulder of her uniform for Angilly. And Pal rank and department iconography are designed to be instantly comprehensible, for both practical and ideological reasons.

"Fellow-Invigilator, Austentarn office, Outreach department," she reports. "Magister." And then actually thinks about what the words mean. Beyond the respectable rank, the office refers to the northern quarter of operations that the Sway is currently operating in, all those little island nations before the ice. And Outreach means…

Her thoughts are shouldered aside by her aunt's next words. "When you take your competences next month, you will achieve a distinction. Or you will not."

Angilly blinks. The logic of the utterance seems inarguable but she detects subtext.

"If you do not," Ostrephy says, "if you are merely *adequate*, or worse, then you should know that in the Fleigh Isles" – meaning a distant part of the Sway that falls within the Austentarn jurisdiction – "they have a mining complex. It runs two miles beneath the level of the sea, and it is where a resentful and subhuman population work out their contribution to general perfection. They have a constant need of new overseers. I understand that you get to see the sun once a month. If, that is, the month is one where the sun gets anywhere past the horizon." And, seeing the *Why?* on Angilly's face, she adds, "I judge this just deep enough to ensure that nobody ever hears that someone of our family was merely *adequate*."

Angilly is gripping the table, not with rage but as though the chasms of the Fleigh Isle' mines might open beneath her at any moment.

"If you achieve a distinction in all subjects, including mathematics, at which I am informed you are not even adequate, then you will receive a Cohort-Invigilator's papers and badge, and I will use my influence to ensure that you receive an appropriate posting." Which nepotism would be, of course, entirely contrary to perfection, but which happens all the time.

"The Invigilators? Correct Appreciation? Magister?" And Angilly can't quite keep the disdain out of her voice. She wanted Correct Speech like her mother. Or Correct Conduct like a soldier, maybe.

Aunt Ostrephy raises an eyebrow sharp as a scimitar. Simultaneously an invitation to speak, and a caution to watch her words.

"Only... plays and entertainment. Censoring *books*. Or the calendar... Or..." And these days Correct Appreciation's love of exact wording means that some of the new sciences like conjuring also come under their remit, but she doesn't take Aunt Ostrephy for a demonist. Not that the woman would need demons to break a niece who had just said something stupid. She meets her aunt's stare defiantly and surprises a tiny spark of humour there, like a candle on a hillside at midnight, a hundred miles away in the rain.

"There are other branches," Ostrephy says. "I also have no time for *theatre*." And Angilly has no objections to actually going to a performance, it's just she didn't much want to atrophy her mind in striking through a line every time some new playwright exceeded the bounds of perfect ideology. "Can you not even tell me what Outreach's remit is?"

Angilly racks her brains and, just as they appear ready to betray her, the answer bobs to the top of her grey matter. "The Diplomatic Office?"

Her aunt's look suggests that her response time there was somewhere south of adequate, but she nods. "And that means?"

Angilly almost rolls her eyes. "Talking to foreigners. The ones we're not ready to fight yet."

She's so fired up with adolescent resentment she isn't quite sure how the moral high ground gets whipped out from under her. Aunt Ostrephy sits back, looking at her with actual contempt. "Adequate," she says. "Just barely. This once I'll place the blame on your curriculum. Your history classes will be replete with accounts of when the troopers marched in, I'm sure. When the liberating armies of the Sway brought enlightenment to one more superstition-ridden and ignorant corner of the world."

Angilly nods warily.

"Let me assure you that, before any of those armies marched, the Diplomatic Office was there first, paving the way. Just as we are there in every imperfect land, disarming those voices that might stir up nations against us, making friends from enemies, changing with a handful of words what the army would need five thousand soldiers to achieve. There are nations who come to us without a single baton discharged, Angilly. There are nations where our troops find the locals thronging to the banner of perfection, eager to overthrow bloody-handed priests and evil magicians and just regular potentates whose currency of rule is nothing but oppression and rapine. There are powerful lands that would once persecute our merchants and strangle our trade and tear perfection from the heart of our conquests, who have become our partners and our friends. And how do these victories come about? The Diplomatic Office. The 'Rain Life', it's been called. By a poet since excised from the canon, but the label remains. Because we are what passes over a nation before the storm comes, putting out fires."

"But that would mean…" Because a new fear has gripped Angilly now. An old fear. Her clutch at the table's edge is born of something different. She smells smoke. "Going abroad."

Aunt Ostrephy's expression is one hundred per cent understanding and zero per cent sympathy. "Did you think that any role you might secure would guarantee you a post on the Archipelago? The Archipelago, with its comforts and its safeties, is a *reward*. It must be *earned*. You were always going abroad, just like all of your classmates. But especially you, Angilly."

Again her face says *Why?*

"Because," Ostrephy says to the unspoken question, "I will not have one of my family live in fear. You will go where you are sent, and you will face the imperfections of that place with a proper Palleseen face on. Because you are born to the greatest nation in the world. Because you are my niece. Because you are Ariet's daughter. Or I will bury you so deep in the earth that nobody on the Archipelago will ever hear the echo of you."

Angilly has a hundred pleas, protests and arguments. They shatter to pieces in her throat before she can speak them, breaking against Aunt Ostrephy's very expression. There is absolutely no give in the woman.

"Your mother died for perfection," she tells Angilly. No mention of her low-ranker father, who died just the same and saved Angilly's life. "I will not have you disgrace that." And, because she has been speaking to Angilly's tutors, she brings up one hand with a squat black taper in it and puts it right in the girl's face. She speaks a word. The tableth set into the base glitters, and the wick sparks into flame.

Angilly screams. But the scream doesn't get any further than her chest. She can feel it there, desperate to ferret its way up to her throat where it can become sound. Because after the garrison she wouldn't even be in a room with a fire, and even now she will always find an excuse to avoid one, endlessly inventive in why any other solution for heat or light is better, or what's so bad about the cold and dark? And she hadn't realised her quirks had been noted.

She stares into the flame and hears screams, smells smoke and her shoulder and arm twinge at her where they were twisted and broken. Her fingers must surely be pressing dents into the wood of the table.

"Breathe," Aunt Ostrephy says, moving the taper closer so that the bridge of Angilly's nose smarts with the heat and her eyebrows wither from it. "I want to see you breathe in and out. Like a Palleseen woman in control of herself, as we always must be. As perfection demands."

Angilly breathes. Stares into the flame. Offering up her memories to it as though she's one of those murderous priests and it's her god. As though she's the burning woman. Trying to turn the searing pain of all those recollections into cold ash.

The flame goes out. Aunt Ostrephy's thumb has shifted the tableth out of place.

"Good," the woman says. "A start. Better than adequate. I will prepare your papers." She stands, stern still. "Two sets of papers. I look forward to seeing which I shall forward with my recommendations to the Assignments office."

The Stick

Sage-Inquirer Meller has a good-natured face and a wicked reputation, as befits the head of the whole Palleseen operation in Farasland. Right now he's doing his bemused act, which Angilly isn't fooled by in the least. It's the conversational equivalent of a gambler's face, waiting to see what the two people across the table do.

In the corner, the birdlike woman in an Accessory's pale uniform waits with pen poised to record everything that is said.

"Well now," he says, a non-standard utterance that won't presumably make it into the final report, "I have before me Fellow-Invigilator Lasaret and Cohort-Invigilator… Angillers?"

"Angilly," she says. "Magister." And she should realise, from that moment. The easy familiarity with which Lasaret's name comes out of Meller's mouth, the pointed stumble over her own, the implicit attention drawn to their disparity in ranks.

But she's nineteen and new-minted and she believes in things, and so she doesn't realise, and soldiers on.

Meller puts on his most pleasant smile, half genial and half vacant and one hundred per cent disingenuous. He looks to the senior of the two up before his desk. "Lasaret, why don't you tell me what this is about?"

Fellow-Invigilator Lasaret has fifteen years on Angilly, but somehow a life in the service has maintained a fragile youth. Aided, she rather thinks, by dye in his hair and some judiciously-applied cosmetics. He lounges, and he has cultivated a little moustache that is absolutely not regulation. He raises his eyebrows at Meller, and then sends them sidelong at Angilly. "I mean," he says lazily, "Sage-Inquirer, it's not my place. It's Angilly's petition, after all."

And that is a tactical error, as far as Angilly is concerned. It *is* her petition, and he should have taken the chance to get in ahead of her. But in his contempt – for her and for the rules – he has cleared the way for her to bring him down.

Meller raises an eyebrow at her. "Cohort-Invigilator, there is a dense report of almost eighty pages on my desk, which I have had the pleasure of perusing. Lasaret, you've…?"

"I have, Magister."

"In which you raise a variety of accusations concerning a senior member of your own school, namely Fellow-Invigilator Lasaret, here present. Very serious accusations."

"Yes, Magister," she confirms.

"And you have seen fit to submit this report direct to me at Correct Speech, the highest point of the landscape, so to speak. Rather than to take the matter up with your own direct superior within your school. The reason for which, I suppose, is that…"

Is that her superior within her school is, of course, Fellow-Invigilator Lasaret. "Is because I consider this a serious-enough matter, with respect to the principles of Correct Thought, that it warranted being brought to your desk," she states.

Meller burlesques a woeful little look at his desk, as if to suggest that the much-abused piece of furniture can't take that many more eighty-page reports. Sage-Inquirer Meller, Angilly reminds herself, has another rather more sturdy item of furniture within his *other* rooms on which he exacts secrets from enemy spies with extreme prejudice, and this woolly act shouldn't be fooling anyone.

"Well the report will be referenced in my final decision should I see fit," Meller says, "but summarise for our notary if you would."

Angilly gives a clipped nod. She has already ordered this part in her head because she knows how these things go. She has even played notary, on occasion, as part of her officer's training. Everyone gets to see a disciplinary or inquest, just to let you know what you're in for if you screw up.

A tiny part of her is savvy enough to tell her she's screwed up but the rest is too callow to admit it.

She stands, arms rigid at her sides, blocking out Lasaret from her peripheral vision. "Over the last two weeks I have observed Fellow-Invigilator Lasaret on numerous occasions consorting with a variety of factions and groups who have no cause to love Correct Thought, or extend a welcome to the Sway. Factions and groups, in fact, that he himself has specifically pledged to the Faraslendi Seat that he will act against, in return for the mercantile and other concessions that Correct Appreciation has been sent here to secure. There is a full list of names, places, times and affiliations in my report, but in summary, I have seen him on very familiar terms with three separate smuggler cartels, including the Red Grieving Bat Society who attacked our supply carrack the *Rectitude* last month. I have seen him meeting with several masked individuals I believe to be part of the dissenting group known as the Whitefish, who are actively attempting to topple the Seat and instal the Jarl-Amir's matrilineal cousin, based on some manner of barbaric prophesy. Worst of all, I spent an entire morning watching the Fellow-Invigilator share a local drink with a man I know to be a priest of the Seadragon cult, a worshipper of a god whose altars run red every spring-tide. A man who will surely be the very first to be purged when we finally bring Farasland into the Sway. Magister."

Meller nods. "Eminently concise, Cohort-Invigilator. Very good. A few follow-up questions, if I may?" And of course he may. He's the most senior Pal officer in a hundred miles. "This extended and detailed period of observation, I note that it requires a junior officer such as yourself to have spent rather a long time in a variety of insalubrious places in the city. I might ask myself what even put you in a position to witness the Fellow-Invigilator in so many compromising meetings."

This she had prepared for. "Magister, I had been tasked with watching for the goods taken from the *Rectitude* when they came to the water-markets. My investigations led me to the Bat, whereupon I observed their meeting with the Fellow-Invigilator. After which I confess to deviating from my brief, and shifting the focus of my time to his activities. Which I hope you will forgive in retrospect, given what I have turned up."

Meller nods again, smiles encouragingly, as at a precocious child who can sing all nine verses of the phalanstery's song. "Let us," he says, "put the matter of forgiveness for exceeding your brief to one side for now."

She swallows. Nods. Meller looks to Lasaret.

"Fellow-Inquirer, this seems like quite a serious business."

"Yes, Magister." Lasaret's still lounging. She dissects his body language for a hint of worry.

"These would appear to be quite unsavoury characters you've been meeting with. Or do you deny it?"

Lasaret casts a sly look at Angilly, and in that moment she understands that of course he can just deny it. Meller has only her word, and Lasaret's word was always going to weigh more.

"I confirm the details of the Cohort-Invigilator's report," he says, and some part of her understands she must be in worse and different trouble than just that, if he won't even bother to call her a liar.

"Well this is very grave," says Meller.

"Might I ask my subordinate a few questions, Magister?" Lasaret asks.

"On the record?"

"Pending future redaction, but yes, Magister." And, at Meller's nod, he goes on, "Cohort-Invigilator Angilly, how did you know that Vortez – the final individual you mentioned – is a priest of the Seadragon cult?"

She blinks at him and he goes on. "You were investigating those Grieving Bat clowns, fair enough, and there was a departmental circular to keep an eye open for those masks the Whitefish use, but Vortez met with me without regalia. Just a shabby, flabby Faraslendi. How did you make him?"

She isn't sure she should be revealing this sort of information to the man who might go advise his priest-murderer friend how to avoid future detection, but Meller plainly expects her to spill it.

"His ears," she says. "The edge of his ears were crimped. The dragon jewellery they wear goes there. He probably had all the right holes and dents elsewhere too. But when his hood came down, I could see his ears." And she sees Lasaret about to say that there's a lot of things that could happen to some Faraslendi's ears, and presses on, "And then I followed him. To the Temple."

Meller and Lasaret exchange a look.

"You followed a man you believed to be a priest of a dangerous and active god," the Sage-Inquirer clarified, "through an effectively lawless part of the city, to a temple known to partake in the sacrifice of locals and foreigners alike."

"Yes, magister. Although spring-tide won't be for another six months."

"Meaning they'd just have had to kill you extempore, I suppose. Well, bring your conclusion, Cohort-Invigilator."

"Magister, I have witnessed my superior consorting, in a friendly manner, with factions who are the enemies of the Sway, either from their actions or their essential natures, as well as with factions whose aims are directly opposed to the parties to whom we are making formal embassies and offers of assistance. I have seen him actively undermining everything our mission here is attempting to achieve. I believe…" The words she will under no circumstance be able to take back, "that he is a traitor to Pallesand, a traitor to Correct Thought. Whether from personal interests or ideological corruption. Hence my forwarding this matter direct to Correct Speech." The Inquirers, the thumb on the hand of the Schools of Correct Thought, that can bend any of the other fingers if it has to.

"Succinctly put," Meller says. "Cohort-Invigilator, how long have you been with us, precisely, here in the Farasland operation?"

"Three weeks, Magister," she says. Two weeks of which she has spent discovering that her superior is a traitor.

"Three weeks. Well, well." His geniality has fallen off his

face and he looks rather sad about things now. She dares to hope. "Fellow-Invigilator, your answer?"

Lasaret nods, considering. "Sage-Inquirer, these meetings all fall under the remit of Outreach's special orders in Farasland. I confirm for the record that they are furthering Palleseen interests in the territory."

For a dreadful moment Angilly thinks that will be *it*. That Lasaret can just say such a thing, and the sheer force of his words will blow her eighty pages out of the window.

"Lasaret," Meller says. And there really is a note of caution there, something other than the chumminess that builds between two men who have worked together for rather longer than three weeks.

"Not for the record," Lasaret says, "but I will provide you with a sealed report to join the dots. You know how it is, with Outreach."

Meller's expression suggests just a slight dissatisfaction with how it is, with Outreach.

"Adjourned pending, then," Meller decides abruptly. "Lasaret, I'm going to ask you to stay in the compound. I appreciate it will impact on your work but Angilly's accusations are serious enough to mandate it. And perhaps you'll actually get your sealed report in within the week."

"Tomorrow, Magister," Lasaret promises.

"Excellent. And Cohort-Invigilator Angilly, you are relieved of duty until we reconvene. Restrict yourself to your quarters or the mess tent. Avoid common areas and you are not to speak a word of this to any other. Understood?"

It is one step off actually being arrested. "Magister?" she barks.

"You have raised a very serious accusation against a senior officer," Meller observes drily. "Did you think you can throw those about like small change and not expect to see an account?"

Thankfully for her sanity, Lasaret is keen to be back out in the world and meeting enemies of the state, so he gets his report in by the end of the day, with the meeting reconvened the next morning. Everyone wants to get this over with as quickly as possible.

The report, being sealed, is not provided to Angilly, nor read out for the notary. It goes from Lasaret's pen to Meller's eye and troubles no other thing in the world.

When the three of them – four with the notary – are back in the Sage-Inquirer's office, the geniality has fallen from the man's face like a corpse from a gallows. He looks serious and humourless and perhaps a little regretful at the waste.

"Let the record show that I have read the Fellow-Invigilator's sealed report and find that it supports his actions, as described by Cohort-Invigilator Angilly, to be within the bounds of Outreach's remit in this territory. Record exoneration of the Fellow, no sanction or censure, no permanent note on his record." All rattled off briskly, so the words leave no bad taste in the mouth that utters them. Angilly stares ahead, stony faced. In the day she's had, waiting incommunicado in her quarters, she has begun to realise what a catastrophic blow she has dealt to her own career in the third week of her first real assignment.

Sage-Inquirer Meller, the man who tortures the spies, but could probably find a spare hour to teach an overreaching subordinate not to trouble his august office with her foolishness, pins her with his stare.

"While it is within my remit to impose penalties and

censure direct to the complainant, in a case found to be without merit, I feel it is more appropriate here to give the privilege to the aggrieved party. Fellow-Invigilator Lasaret, this individual is within your department. You have full control over her. I suggest you exert it as you see fit."

"Thank you, Magister," Lasaret says smoothly, and stands, so as not to take up any more of Meller's valuable time. "Cohort-Invigilator." He clicks his fingers and she jolts to her feet. "My office. Wait for me there."

He keeps her waiting. Lasaret's office is, she thinks, a shrine to the incorrect. There are bits and pieces of local colour all over the walls: masks and weapons, a reptilian hunting trophy, the Faraslendi tapestries that show weird chains of people and animals turning into one another. The grate around the fire that Lasaret's aide has banked up against the chill is ornate, twisted sea-creatures and wrack in wrought iron. Over it, a ragged banner with a finned and serpentine shape, the Seadragon of the cult. And perhaps that's what the man worships. Perhaps his corruption runs that deep.

She has, she understands, managed to do absolutely the right thing in absolutely the wrong way. Maybe she could have written to her aunt, or have her words reach some Sage within Correct Appreciation who'd be willing to interfere in the matter. Or maybe she could have gathered more evidence, as if that would have helped. Caught Lasaret bloody to the elbows over an altar. Or just filling his pockets with bribes from the smugglers and pirates.

But she didn't. She did things the correct way. She wrote a report and petitioned the appropriate authority. And now, in retrospect, too late, she can see how the correct way of doing things was also absolutely the wrong way. And she, young, brash, committed, desperate to make something of herself, has just made a mess.

Lasaret enters the office. He's taken the time to change, she sees. In fact he's wearing that non-regulation long sea coat she's seen him in, about the water-markets and docks. He is, she divines, going to tie off the loose end that is *her*, before going on to warn his foreign friends.

She has a knife, of course. Standard soldier's accoutrement. And it's not her duelling foil, but she's had basic training, and a lot of the fencing footwork carries over. If any of this registers in her body language, Lasaret overlooks it. He crosses close enough to her for a stabbing and then throws himself down in the chair behind his desk. He actually puts his boots up on the surface, meaning if she does want to stab him, he's made it very easy for her.

He holds up a big bundled sheath of papers. "Know what this is, Angilly?"

She keeps her face stony. "My report, Magister." All eighty hard-written pages.

He begins feeding pages into the fire. Reaching back until his hand feels the right heat, then releasing them in flurries of three or four. So absurdly insouciant that she'd have laughed under literally any other circumstances.

"Yes and no," he says. Another handful of accusations start to crisp and char. "It is indeed your report and petition. It is also the official record of the entire meeting." Meaning not just her hard work but that of the notary. He wants not a trace of the whole incident left in writing. The only evidence that anyone pointed the finger at Fellow-Invigilator Lasaret will be the sudden dismissal of Angilly from her post.

Probably there's still a deep mine somewhere that wants an overseer.

"I want you to listen to me," Lasaret tells her. "This is what was in my sealed report to Meller. The smuggling societies, that have been such a drag on our shipping, are also the most efficient way to move goods in and out of the city. They have complete fiat. No official channel can stop them. And yes, in the long term, that's a problem. When Farasland is within the Sway and there's a Perfector governing the city, we'll need to crack down on all of that. But right *now* they make very useful partners, because there are *plenty* of things that we, Outreach, want to bring into the city that we don't want to trouble the Seat with. And when the time comes to crush the Red Grieving Bat and all the rest of them, we'll have cosied up with them so much that we'll practically know the shoe size of every last one of their ship captains." From a desk drawer he fishes out a regulation tin cup and a flask, and pours a solitary drink. "The Whitefish Insurgency is going to be a problem in about a year," he says, as though he's some heathen oracle. "The Jarl-Amir isn't popular, which means that a remarkable spectrum of factions and people are looking at his cousin-in-exile and weighing up their self-interest. Does the Sway care which barbarian wears the big hat and reclines on that rather ugly couch, Angilly?"

"We have made pledges to—"

"Answer my question, as a point of ideology," he tells her, another fist of crumpled papers crackling behind the ornate grate.

"No, Magister. Not solely from ideology."

"And from pragmatism?"

"We have made pledges to—"

"The Faraslendi Seat offers us the most trivial concessions for all the pledges we have made, because we are not relevant in the Jarl-Amir's world," Lasaret says. "The Whitefish and their pretender are the underdogs, desperate to triumph against a state that remains stable and secure enough to see off their best efforts. Unless, of course, they had the support of a strong external ally. And just think what they might agree to, in order to gain such support. Why, we might almost secure the entire state for perfection without a fight. Palleseen advisors, ordinances, the lot, and not a penny in tax for our merchants." And he lets the last of the pages go.

"And the priest?" she asks. "Magister."

"Ah, well, my old friend Vortez," Lasaret says, with a self-deprecating smile. "Is that really your most pressing question?"

It is not. The thing she really needs to ask is, "Why are you telling me this?"

He's youngest when he grins. "You mean, am I putting you in a position where you know so much I'd have to kill you, or do I just enjoy showing you how very clever I am? Or possibly I, a fallen officer gone rogue, still feel the need to justify myself to my crusading subordinate?" And he holds her gaze, and she can't tell even the least iota of what he's thinking. She realises she'd never before met anyone whose face is such a born liar.

"Magister," she says heavily, "just get to it. I can see I'm fucked, here. I stand by everything I did, but the rot's so deep here it'll drown me. So fine. So let's just get to it. Magister." Clenching her fists, and one of them surreptitiously close to her knife-hilt, which he still hasn't registered as a threat.

"Ah yes. Your fate," he agrees pleasantly, toying with the tin cup. "I'm bringing you onto my team. A sideways shift, no promotion for you yet, but you've only been here three weeks after all."

The shift of direction is so sudden she can't breathe for a second. "Magister?"

"Your report was very good," he says. "Bit of a shame it's somehow been mislaid, really. Very thorough, excellent attention to detail. Clear and concise. Good tradecraft, good logic. And obviously you went considerably beyond your personal remit, in order to gather that information. Which in many cases doesn't attract the good kind of notice from your superiors, but where the other departments build their forts and sheds, we in Outreach pitch tents, Angilly. And the thing about tents is that they have stretchy walls and they move around a lot. Also, you put some considerable effort into how you followed me around, and I appreciate that."

She feels a plunge of anger at her own failings. "You saw me."

"I made you out, yes," he said. "But I don't think any of the worthies I was meeting did. You got the clothes right. You kept changing outfits, day to day. The status-marks you drew on your forehead were situationally appropriate. You did your homework, basically. There's still a lot of the phal and the drill ground in the way you walk, though. That's something you need to work on. And all this from someone who's not had any brief for covert work. First principles. Very impressive."

He produces a second tin cup from the drawer and fills it before her disbelieving eyes.

"But more than that, you followed Vortez to his *temple*, and that's something he's not let me do, and I've been angling at it for over a month. Because the Seadragon cult is dangerous and influential, and if we make our move we're either going to have to bite our tongues and work with them, or we're going to have to go in with fire and baton and clear them out when they're all there next spring-tide."

"Work with—?"

"Not my preferred option," and all the lounging is gone from him. "And only in the short term. Because they are exactly the sort of thing perfection cannot co-exist with for long. But it's a possibility, if the timing doesn't work or if we don't think we can root them out completely. Because that's the sort of judgment call Outreach has to make. The final call will be from some Sage-Monitor at the head of our liberation force, but they've learned to listen to us. Most of them. Do you understand me, Angilly?"

He pushes the full tin cup across the desk to her. Behind him, the last of her carefully-chosen words go up in smoke. "Outreach needs to be able to flex. We need to be able to see the world from an imperfect point of view. Not just understand it, but *appreciate* it. Incorrect Appreciation. That's why they give the job to the Invigilators, perhaps. For the record, I do genuinely like Vortez. As a person, not a priest. A man of many qualities. Have him born on the Archipelago, he'd be an asset. Probably be here in my boots giving you your orders. If there was any way I could sever him from his faith and redeem him, I would do." A brooding look, and perhaps this once she's seeing the real man behind the pliable features. "But I don't think I'll win that battle. And so he'll have to go, sooner or later. And I'll regret it, and that regret won't make it into my final report, and then I, and Outreach and Correct Appreciation, will move on. As will you. And perhaps by then we can get you that promotion. Because you, Angilly, have potential. Just as soon as you can do something about that stick."

"Stick, Magister?" she asks blankly.

"The one up your arse." His rejuvenating grin comes back and he raises his cup. "To a long and productive career, Angilly. And for Reason's sake take your hand away from your knife. Nobody's getting stabbed today."

Ashes and Sparks

When the order came, to board ship for Jarokir, she didn't want to go. Nobody asked, of course. The point of 'orders' is that her consent isn't required. She didn't even consider any option other than complying. She's a Companion-Invigilator with a bright career ahead of her as aide to Fellow-Invigilator Lasaret. That's what's important. That she's returning to the land where they burned her parents alive is incidental. Personal problems, that are never allowed to get in the way of the Palleseen Sway's demands.

Gone from having prospects to being a rising star with that promised promotion in her pocket. At year's end last year she dined with stern Aunt Ostrephy and the old woman had barely disapproved of her *at all*.

The old heat hits her, when she steps out. Not the fire heat, not the close and airless heat of the rainy season, but the heat of all the other times she'd been in Jarokir. The base-level dry bake of the place, that turns everything to kindling.

Lasaret fans at his face with his cap. Four years has added a surprising amount of weight to him. A capable aide means more time for him behind a desk. Successful operations in Farasland and the Torne Islands mean more approval from on high, which for him translates into a certain love of fine dining. A handful of particularly hard choices, who to betray, who to support, meant that those tin cups and the flask of strong drink came out from the desk drawer more and more often, but it hasn't taken away his edge. Just means that he can only enjoy his successes and commendations after they've steeped a little in rum.

The Jarokiri plantations turn out good rum, Angilly hears. Doubtless Lasaret will gift them his expert opinion.

She, Lasaret and the new boy, Cohort-Invigilator Tomelly. A travelling task force recently returned from delving into a resurgence of the Boat Cult amongst the dockers at the big Torne shipyards. And that might sound like it would be all thumbscrews and executions, but Lasaret hasn't lost his subtle touch. What had once been a dread cult worshipping benthic monstrosities beyond human comprehension had become just a social club. Not exactly within the bounds of perfection, but right now it would cause more disruption to crack down on it than to allow the locals to enjoy their little peculiarities. The de-godded cult as a safety valve means ships get built and refitted and supplied on their way across to the rich territories on the far side of the sea. Like Jarokir.

The statlos who meets them at the dock has every button of his uniform in the right hole, tight at the neck and the cuffs and the knees, and he's already gone the colour of cooked lobster. Lasaret's uniform is already undone everywhere except the codpiece, flapping about him like motley. Angilly's buttoned hers back and opened her shirt a few notches. Tomelly, the new boy, isn't confident enough to follow suit yet. He's full of the dignity of his position, and she can remember when she was just like that.

She remembers the garrison.

In fact, her memory is the only place it exists. Eleven years of liberation have seen the entire neighbourhood re-edified. From a walled compound with a handful of hastily thrown-up and defensible buildings – too defensible, in fact – to regular streets, cobbled and mortared so the rains won't sweep them into the sea, a grid of stone buildings that are half repurposed local architecture and half the squat and honestly unlovely things that Pal colonial architects tend to throw up. Beyond them, Port Urchen had been a relatively modest port town and is now pushing for city status. The old temple district is now where the merchants keep their factoras, business premises and townhouses. Beyond that are the mills and warehouses and refineries, and a vast and uneven landscape of shacks and shanties where the locals have filtered in from the countryside because here's where the work is. Or been marched in at baton-point if the work outweighs the volunteers. That the work gets done is a major precept of perfection.

Still, there *is* work, and what would all those locals be doing with their time otherwise? Something unproductive, no doubt. Propitiating gods, probably.

When she enters the new garrison building – bigger windows, less defensible, more like a place people actually live – she smells smoke, just for a moment. Actually stops at the threshold so that Lasaret looks back at her. And the extra flesh on his face just makes him harder to read, so she doesn't know if he understands that brief hesitation. Then Tomelly treads on her heels and she crosses inside, and soon after the three of them are in an airy office, tall windows with the shutters thrown wide and just a mesh across to keep the biggest bugs out. A desk, Pal standard for officers of Fellow rank. Pigeonholes and shelves ready to file reports in. The usual.

Lasaret gets out his flask and three cups, of which two are filled, Tomelly being an abstainer. Not a quality that exactly makes the new boy beloved, but on the other hand he's barely twenty and probably wouldn't be able to take the strong stuff his superior prefers. Angilly, who's been building up a tolerance for four years, knocks hers back.

"Tom, you're with me on this one. Shadows and footsteps, best way to learn," Lasaret says. "You read the brief on the ship? Or were you too busy hurling out the porthole?"

Tomelly doesn't do that furious blush he did when he first joined the team. He's learned to master his face that much, at least. "I read it, Magister." Essentially some concerns over relations between local magnates and the Palleseen body mercantile. A few worries that what seems on the surface to be just the usual jockeying over money might hide something a little more cultish. Jarokir had been a land of a thousand temples, before its liberation. A rich and convoluted tapestry of gods. A tradition of energetic proselytising. Everywhere the Palleseen had sought to export their perfection, they had met their opposite numbers from this Jarokiri temple or that, spouting sectarian doctrine. Until a full-on campaign against Jarokir had been the only answer. The fiercest fight the Palleseen army had committed to, and most of the embattled faiths hadn't gone quietly. Not even when their sacred places had been torn open and raided for decantable magic. Rogue religious terrorists had continued to plague the liberating forces for years. As Angilly knew.

That was mostly gone by now, they said. A handful of holdouts, little more than bandits with a holy book or thurible stashed at the bottom of their packs. Other than that, Jarokir had become one of the great wealth-baskets of the Palleseen Sway. Spices and sugar, paper and passable tea.

"We're going to talk to some of the local big lads," Lasaret tells Tomelly. "Just remember they were all slavering votaries devouring human flesh just a few years back and we'll get on fine." That old grin of his, at the kid's discomfort, but the boy's learning fast. Shadows and footsteps, like Lasaret says. Only so much you can learn from a book or in the phal. You need to see it done in the field.

"You'll also be my liaison with Angilly, because she is going to be on her own recognizance over here. You're good with that?" He fixes her with a suddenly steady eye and she realises he'd understood that moment of doubt at the threshold, after all.

"Of course, Magister," she says coolly.

"Good. Because you get to play nursemaid, among other things. New member of the team. Companion-Invigilator Benallers should be around here. He's from some outfit called Exceptional Stratagems, which sounds suspect as anything and is so new nobody's gotten around to telling me what they're about. I have no idea what he's good for, but make sure you show him who's in charge. I'm not having some bookish prig foisted on us and ordering my people around. While you're wrangling *him*, I've got a list of our people to get in with, to see if the problem's coming from our side." Because it's almost certainly the locals who are going to get their knuckles rapped and their taxes raised, but it never hurts to make sure there isn't someone from Correct Exchange egregiously lining their own pockets.

"Ben*ay*ers," says the man.

Angilly blinks. "Say again?"

"Ben*ay*ers," he repeats smoothly. Companion-Invigilator Benallers is someone who does most things smoothly, she reckons. Certainly he's very smooth on the eye, while at the same time being someone the phrase 'non-regulation' might have been coined for.

She flicks her gaze to the papers Lasaret gave her. "Not what it says here," she notes mildly. "You should get that changed at Records."

Around them, the murmur of a decently informal officer's mess rises and falls, the staff of the garrison and a score of visitors from the merchant town dining and drinking, and some old girl at the far end reading out the most recent news dispatches in a nasal voice. They're all exactly as Angilly would expect, for Palleseen expats who've been out here for a few years. Uniforms worn loose, the occasional piece of local colour. Open Pal collars revealing a flash of the bright Jarokiri neck-scarves, glittering with metal threads and tiny semiprecious stones. Wearable wealth always fashionable with anyone who's been a soldier.

Benallers isn't any of that. He's only been in Port Urchen a week, waiting for his comrade Invigilators to catch up with him. His jacket is slung on the back of his chair and his shirt is undone by a couple of buttons. It's the most positively indecent thing Angilly has ever seen. She wants to report him for subverting the whole concept of military costume.

He has a long face and very pale skin. The bluish shadow of stubble on his cheeks and chin suggests he hasn't shaved for three days, but she'll learn soon enough that it materialises within an hour of the razor's passage like clouds following the sun. His eyes are ice blue, his features *aristocratic* in some way she can't quite place. And foreign. A great deal there that hasn't come out of the Palleseen Archipelago for sure, and yet here he is in the dark uniform of an officer.

He hasn't taken those chill eyes off her, and his bold, frank stare is making her squirm. There's something unnatural about him. No, there are several unnatural things about him, and she can only account for some of them.

"Outreach," he says. "I always fancied that. So much nicer to talk to people before you shoot them."

"Yes. It makes you really fulfilled when you fire your baton," she says. "What the hell is Exceptional Stratagems?"

Benallers smiles, self-deprecating, a little embarrassed. "Would you believe me if I just said it was dirty tricks and espionage?" His expression invites her into a conspiracy of unknown parameters.

"Well, not now you've put it like that."

"Oh well, it's nothing. It's ridiculous. You'll laugh. Why don't we just assume I'm here to redact Jarokiri literature or something, and get on with our work. Work which, I shouldn't need to say, my speciality won't be of any use for."

She can't make him out, not quite. It isn't that he's an inveterate layerer of expressions, like Lasaret, whose career has taught him a thousand ways to obfuscate his true thoughts. It's that Benallers' face – Ben*ay*ers, as he pronounces it – is written partly in a script she simply can't translate.

They spend that afternoon talking to three separate trade factors from Correct Exchange who complain that the local merchants have gotten uppity with them, are shorting them on supply, giving them inferior goods. They don't want the velvet glove of Outreach. They want Correct Conduct and a bunch of troopers with batons to go re-establish just who is supposed to be dictating to whom here in occupied – *liberated* – Jarokir. Angilly does the talking, and Benallers sits beside her radiating a curious kind of menace. She doesn't feel it herself, but she sees the effects of it. When some Companion-Broker starts making demands and giving orders, Benallers shifts in his seat and looks up from flicking at the lint on his sleeve. The bolshy Broker abruptly reconsiders their relative status and starts listening to Angilly instead of talking over her. And Angilly, who's had four years' intensive training in subtext and body language, isn't quite sure how he does it.

That evening she exchanges scribbled reports with Tomelly, then shares intel with her new partner over some of the local rum.

"I'm going to say something now," she tells Benallers carefully. "And it's a bit of a stretch, and you're welcome to laugh at me." And she finds she actually doesn't want him to laugh at her. That long, exotic face of his looks purpose-made for it, and she feels it would cut. But still nothing ventured… "Exceptional Stratagems is magic. You're a magician." Having watched him in action for half a day it's the only thing that made sense.

And she has him. She sees his face stop, that ease freezing on his features. A moment of vulnerability puncturing his defences as though she bound under his guard and got him in the ribs just as he thought he had the measure of her.

"Tell me, what sort of a name is Benallers?" She looks at him over the rim of her cup.

"Allorwen," he tells her, over his own, matching her pose perfectly. "From my mother. My father was a Sage-Archivist, if that restores your trust in me at all. And yes, Exceptional Stratagems is magic, of a sort. Although not what you're thinking of, or I'd be over in Correct Erudition with ink on my fingers."

Which is a valid point. What sort of magician gets assigned to Correct Appreciation, whose interest is not the old books of yesteryear but the new pages of today: literature, laws, treaties…

Contracts, of course. As much as the Brokers of Correct Exchange, Correct Appreciation loves a well-drafted contract. And she casts her mind back to what little she knows of Allor, just one more unperfected nation on the far side of the sea from Jarokir.

After the silence between them has stretched out too long, he brings out a neatly folded-over and tape-bound document, that looks like nothing so much as a set of legal pleadings. "Have a look," he invites. "Sate your curiosity on the forbidden depravities of a heathen tradition."

And he smiles, and she smiles back, but her hands shake ever so slightly when she takes it, undoes the bindings and reads.

What astonishes her, really, was how mundane so much of it is. The form, the structure of the language, just like any other binding agreement one might need to commit to writing. She's seen a hundred of them. If one overlooks the peculiar terminology and definitions, words and symbols that make her uneasy just to see them. Dangerous things. Unsound things. Touched with a curious attraction, therefore.

Benallers leans back in his chair, watching her. And he's working very hard not to care, but she can see him sieving her for a reaction. Braced for it. His face, more open than he means it, holds with a curious attraction. The allure of forbidden things. Forbidden and, simultaneously, given a uniform and a new-minted department name and sent out to serve the Palleseen Sway.

"Demons." Her eyebrows high, but only in a *What has the world come to?* sort of a way. Determined to take it in her stride.

"Eleven pages of subclauses, provisos and small print,"

Benallers confirms. "If there was ever a branch of arcana more suited to the Palleseen administration I don't know what it is."

The laugh surprises her, as though it, too, has been conjured up by his magic. It breaks the reserve she's been carefully building. She snorts, inhales some rum unwisely, and that's how a wicked conjurer of entities from the Realms Below ends up slapping her on the back as she coughs her lungs out in the officer's mess.

She wants to ask if she can see his demons, but that would sound absolutely like some sort of proposition. And, honestly, if she's going to go there, she might as well just say it openly. Which, given that by then they've adjourned to his quarters, she does. Because one of the benefits of perfection is the demystifying of human relationships, and she has learned to take opportunities where she can.

"Fellow-Invigilator Lasaret told me to make sure you know who's in charge," she tells him.

Benallers cocks an eyebrow at that, in a way that suggests she's welcome to try.

"Basically it's the relic trade," says Cohort-Broker Woret. He's a skinny little man whose domain is deep in in the storerooms beneath the garrison building, the last name on Angilly's list. They've spoken to the representatives of half a dozen merchant factoras, all of whom feel they're being stiffed by the locals. Lasaret – in his persona as a crooked officer panhandling for bribes – has spoken to half a dozen representatives of Jarokiri clans who feel they're being stiffed by the Pals. Which would probably just be business as usual if the Pals they're pointing at weren't also complaining.

There's some shadowed shape moving underneath all of the finger-pointing, like a shark in shallow water. Angilly smells smoke, and she doesn't like it.

And the old fire cult is cold ash now, they say. Along with most of the other militant sects that wouldn't take liberation lying down. Had a good run of it, maybe, but there's a decade-and-change down the river since the war, and the Pals absolutely prioritised extinguishing the Jarokiri religions, dismantling their structures and ruthlessly desecrating their holy places. And when that sparked outrage in the populace, they lined those sections of the populace against the wall and taught them the foolishness of clinging on to old superstitions through the baton and the lash. The first decade of Jarokiri liberation was a constant round of brutal retaliation and that's why we have Outreach now. But, in the interim, at least nobody's getting burned alive for the gods any more and that is surely a good thing.

"They're still finding the odd temple they missed," says Woret. "Plus all the safe-houses and cellars-turned-shrines that happened when the priests got moved on the first few times. Each one filled with Gabble." That old soldier's slang for valuable-but-religious loot that might get you up before Correct Speech if it was found in your pack. "Magic stuff," Woret adds. "The Decanters love it. The Archivists love it. Plus there are collectors, you know. Always a market. Anyway, that's your problem here. The locals want it cos half of them are still heathens on the side. The factors want it because they're never happy with how full their boots are." Woret has a refreshingly direct, candid approach to the functioning of the Palleseen Sway. If they ever drummed ideology into him in the phal, then actual service washed it out of his system long ago. He's a decade older than Angilly and Benallers, a rank lower, and utterly unconcerned about any of that. He hasn't *magister*ed them once, and by unspoken agreement they haven't stood on ceremony. Nor does Benallers spook him.

Woret shrugs at the wickedness of a world still in need of perfection. A whole secret war between locals and Pals over who gets their grubby hands on the residue of a score of dead religions. Not cultists but profiteers. And here's poor Woret just trying to do his job. Shrugging the sort of sloped shoulders that blame just sloughs past and never finds purchase on.

But people like Woret hear a great deal, and he gives them names on both sides, the worst culprits, people they can set down in the reports they'll forward to Correct Speech. Because Outreach won't be putting the screws on anyone, but they can certainly stitch you up for the Inquirers if they're so minded.

They meet with Tomelly again. Tomelly frowns down his nose at Benallers, feeling his place as third in the triumvirate usurped. Ambitious, like every kid fresh out of the phalanstery. She hands over Woret's list, and receives a summary of Lasaret's closing activities. His final interviews. Nothing that contradicts Woret's insights into the situation here in Port Urchen. Nothing that absolutely confirms it, either, but still...

Not in composing her report, but in handing it over to Tomelly, does she feel slightly dissatisfied. A mess, really. Everyone on the take. Exactly what she'd expect to find after ten years of relative peace and profit. Imperfection creeping in – not the local ecclesiastical kind but just the regular sort that the Pals create for themselves, and must be constantly vigilant against. Really very exactly what she'd expect to find.

They compare notes later, she and Benallers. Angilly's unfinished final report sitting, lukewarm and still cooling, on the desk in her borrowed quarters. Compared, and found the same note sitting towards the forefront of both of their minds. That it was exactly what either of them would have expected to find. Submit names, Correct Speech raps a few knuckles and maybe pulls out a fingernail or two if matters turn out to be worse. All's right with the world.

"Of course, if you wanted," Benallers says, by the light of a lantern turned down low, "we could dig."

"We've dug." He's warm beside her. Digging sounds like hard work. Then, a suspicion: "Or do you mean…?"

She feels him breathe in, long, slow. Hold it, for a moment, before letting it out. A man opening the gates of a fortress to someone he hopes isn't an enemy. "One of the advantages to nobody knowing what the hell Exceptional Stratagems means is that nobody knows how to guard against it," he says. She wonders if there's a barb in that remark meant for her. "Some of the cults here used demons. It's usually a hard one-way-or-the-other, with temples." And by now she's learned that, over in Allor, it's the one way: that demons are their religion, no gods at all.

"What of it?"

"When the cults go away, the demons can get left behind."

"This sounds outside your remit."

"Not at all. The demons don't care about the cults, not really. One master or another, they don't care if there's a god behind it. The contract is all. If you thought that Outreach would condone it, I could conjure up something that used to do service in some temple or other. Sniff out some relics."

And she doesn't really care about the relics. The thought of having some ancient sacred tat in hand, to add weight to

Woret's list of names, does not excite her. Seeing Benallers do his thing, ply his filthy unsound trade, *that* excites her. Because it's sat there between them, his speciality, inextricably tied up with the foreignness of him and the way he corrects how people say his name, but like all private, obscene things he's kept it decently covered up until now.

It makes him dangerous. It makes him wicked. She finds she likes that. "Do it," she says.

Honestly, it's not as dangerous or wicked as she thought. There's no blood sacrifice, not even of something small like a chicken. He does use a magic circle, but it's just a matter of rolling the rug back and drawing it on the floor in chalk. Like children in a playground except some deep part of her will absolutely not walk across it or scuff the markings, and if this was her permanent room she'd have the flooring replaced after he was done. And he hums to himself as he's doing it, and possibly it's an infernal hum from the depths of the abyss but it just sounds like one of those soldiers' marching songs you get ear wormed to death with after you've been on assignment with the regular army even once.

Then he looks up at her, crouched there on the balls of his feet, one hand to the floorboards and the other clutched about the chalk, and the lantern catches his eyes. They gleam like an animal's.

The air charges like a tableth. The chalk marks don't flare or glow but abruptly she can't focus on them properly. He is conjuring a demon. The bared wood within the circle seems to extend downwards forever, its coarse grain the topography of a blasted wasteland country.

The demon, when it arrives, is terrifying. Because he

didn't specify which cult it had originally been attached to, and he doesn't know her past, and it's on fire. A thing like a human form aflame, running like wax so that the bones are constantly being revealed, yet never melting away. Its eyes are wide and terrified and her father's; its mouth is full of black and charred teeth. It makes its face into Benallers' own, his skin peeling and his flesh dripping. A word from him has it flinching back, spitting like a pan, becoming just Aggregate-of-Humanity rather than anyone in particular.

Angilly holds herself rigid. And this isn't the blazing woman she remembers, from That Day. But it smells of her. It has the taint of the same sect about it.

Benallers watches her. For a moment she thinks he knows all, and is doing this because he hates her and wants her to suffer. Then she knows that what she's looking into, right then, is a mirror. Perhaps a mirror the demon brought with it. The person that hates her and wants her to suffer is her, deep down. The girl reborn from her parents' ashes. Nothing rational about it, but still.

She meets the demon's gaze. Sets her jaw. Clutches the hilt of her knife in that way she has, that has alarmed a variety of people over the years. "Can I speak to it?"

"With me here, yes. It is my will that it answer you truthfully."

"Thing," she addresses the demon. A certain weariness in its agonised eyes suggests this isn't the first time it's been referred to as such. "Somewhere near here is the regalia of your past masters," she tells it. "Do you understand me?"

"I scent the trappings of divinity." It speaks very carefully around its cracked and crumbling teeth, its diction exaggerated. Weirdly, that makes it less frightening, more into the realms of a human dealing with a disability. She can see its melting face constantly turning into her own and then forcing itself into that bland neutral country of nobody-in-particular. As though its warped reflections are not demonic cruelty at all, but just something it does when it isn't really paying attention.

"Can you lead us to them?" she asks.

"Yes," it says, and makes no move to do so, because demons are demons and they don't exactly volunteer services to those that bind them.

She confers briefly with Benallers over how best to phrase the instruction, and then commands the demon to do her bidding, second hand. It is a weird thrilling, proscribed thing, even though it's being done under cover of the uniform. *See how we turn the tools of superstition back on their masters!* And after all, isn't this grey area what Outreach is all about? Benallers' particular brand of mischief fits right in.

There is such a thing as a pro forma contract for a demon, she discovers. Benallers writes in names and details and he and the demon both seal it with their marks. The thing steps from the circle. It leaves greasy, waxy footprints that evaporate after a few heartbeats. There are, Benallers explains, subclauses devoted to ensuring the taint of the Realms Below cleans up after itself.

Weirdly reduced, thin and miserable, its infernal agonies muted, the demon shuffles off to show them where the relics are. And that's where they find Tomelly's body.

They're down under the garrison itself, though the vaulted architecture suggests this is a sub-cellar of the Jarokiri temple stronghold they knocked down to build it. Everything thoroughly desanctified of course, a top-grade desecration from the masters of the art, but that's the problem with rats. They creep back in.

Tomelly lies in a blackened circle and there's another blackened circle, or at least concavity, where his heart should be. A crisp-edged scooped-out hole in the centre of his chest. They teach you that, in basic medicine in the phal. The heart sounds like it's to the left, but that's just the stronger side of it, the fiercer beat. Mostly the heart's in the centre. Angilly remembers thinking *What a useless piece of information* at the time, and here she is, finding a use for it after all.

She wastes one half-second thinking this might have been Benallers. It looks like demon work, at first glance. The circle, the sacrifice. Except circles are basic geometry and there are more things you might sacrifice to than demons. And Benallers has said, at least, that the conjuration manual they're developing for regular military use has no truck with human souls as currency. Not humanitarianism so much as the whole business stinking a little much of superstition.

Besides, she recognises the scrawled markings. They were on the watch sheet that Lasaret received on the ship, but, more than that, they were the ones she saw in the air dancing around the blazing woman, the priestess who was setting the very rain on fire. The flaming cult. The one they were supposed to have put out.

That is what they see. Perhaps that is what they are supposed to see. But she sees one thing more.

"Backwards," she says. Because it was eleven years ago, but she has seen these symbols in their natural habitat. She might even be the only person in Port Urchen who has, given how staff get rotated in and out. She saw them blaze in air, and even though the blazing woman turned and stalked away, those sigils looked the same *from every side*. That was the *sacred* of them, that you couldn't write them backwards even if you tried. Except someone has here.

And the error didn't save Tomelly. The ritual still worked. But that's because gods aren't ever as finicky or particular as their priests like people to believe.

"This is amateur work," she says, and then, "Tomelly had our list. The names. Why is he here?" And then, before Benallers can speculate, "He was an ambitious kid, like they all are." Like she'd been, when she had Lasaret hauled up before the Inquirers that time. "He didn't just want to play messenger."

Benallers says, "He wanted the commendation. But he's not dead on Merchant Row and he's not dead out in the workers' town. What else was in your report?"

"Where the information came from," Angilly notes. Meaning the source of all those names. A source Tomelly might have returned to, to squeeze a little more from. And discovered a little too much. The source. Here. The garrison stores.

They both hear the hiss of breath as Woret works out it's not going to wash. When he steps out, his hands are on fire. The sigils, in the air, are the right way round, but when he was drawing them on the ground the fires were out and he'd have been doing it from memory. Such odd little things that trip us up. Of course, right then she isn't thinking about any of that because his *hands* are on *fire*.

On fire.

He has a big amulet about his neck, polished bronze that glimmers and sears. Some sacred whatnot torn from the temple of the sacred flame and passed hand to hand from one dealer in dubious antiquities to the next, rather than drained of its potency by the Decanters.

"All that work," Benallers says, "getting us to go chase your competitors, and you go and make the poor kid look like a ritual sacrifice. What, he found you packing it all away so you could make it disappear before we came looking for it? Caught you in the act? And this was your best shot? Send us haring off after a long-dead fire cult."

Woret snarls, his lips working. And probably Benallers is right. Probably Woret just has some cult tat with enough of a spark in it to kill Tomelly, and the two of them as well. Probably the extinguished fire cult designed all their sacred artefacts for a layman's ease of use. But she looks into the storeman's face and sees something glimmer there. Something banned. Something sacred. Handle the artefacts of divinity enough and something nasty and sticky rubs off on your fingers, like molten tar. Most likely Woret thought he was setting a false trail pointing at a dead cult, but that doesn't mean it wasn't a ritual sacrifice *as well*.

The fire leaps with malign intent in Woret's hands. His face is that of a man whose profiteering has already accelerated into murder and is on the verge of becoming a colossal act of conflagratory destruction. He can't control it, because it's in him like a fever. Angilly smells smoke and this time it's because there is smoke. Smoke conjured from nowhere to please a vanished god.

She has her knife out and goes for him. It's not courage. It's terror. Lunging at Woret, into the flames, is marginally more bearable than just standing there. Or than fleeing and leaving Benallers to his fate.

The fire flares in her face. She's twelve again. She freezes, mid-strike. Woret is howling something and maybe it's madness and maybe the madness is divinely mandated, the last revenge of a trivialised god. She's going to burn. She's going to burn like her parents did. It's what she owes Jarokir and the world.

The demon gets in the way. A clause she hadn't realised was in Benallers' contract. And what use is a wax demon against a fire, exactly. Except if wax really burned then what use would a candle be? Instead the thing runs and howls and pools on the floor but keeps reforming, because everyone knows demons are things of fire too. And Woret howls right back, and while he's hollering into his own glossy, dripping face she darts around the side and puts her knife in up to the hilt. And then eighteen more times, in an act that Lasaret will characterise as 'being thorough' and not 'fear-driven frenzy'.

The fires go out. The last embers of the god spending themselves in chewing at the edges of Woret's fingernails. She comes to herself with every muscle dancing, shaking with spent emotion. Well spent, though. Coin she won't get back. She doesn't even jump when Benallers puts his hand on her shoulder. Just leans into him when he puts his arms round her. And neither Woret's profiteering nor his madness had much to do with what happened a decade ago in the old garrison building they've long-since torn down, but somehow she feels she's revenged herself for what happened back then, even so.

Foxes

"I'm getting the impression," Angilly says over the crowd's building murmur, "that they hate demons here, Ben."

Beside her, Benallers grimaces. "Here? Here they just dislike demons. You should try Usmai. In Usmai they *really* hate demons."

"Can you send the thing back?"

The *thing* in question is a hunched, prickle-skinned thing with tattered, cropped wings. Like a lot of Benallers' conjurations, it's a bloodhound for certain magics, but its snuffling has led them out into a market here in central Magnelei and abruptly everyone's shouting at them. And while few sane people relish a leashed demon turning up out of the blue, apparently there's a whole business about everyone's goods suddenly being ritually unclean that nobody mentioned in the cultural brief. And Bracite traditional dress includes single-edged knives thrust through the belt, many of which are now pugnaciously in hand.

"If we send it back then there's just us and them," Benallers points out.

"Good point," Angilly admits and, at this point, reinforcements turn up, being a squad of soldiers in familiar charcoal grey plus a handful of Accessories. Matters teeter on the edge of those nasty knives, then. Bracinta is not within the Sway, after all. The Pals have a significant presence here, but not a controlling one. If the whole city erupts in anti-perfection riots, there aren't enough batons for anything other than a quick retreat.

Thankfully, Benallers does vanish away his demon at that point and, in the absence of the inciting entity and the presence of Palleseen discipline, the crowd begins to subside. A handful of itinerant priests or magicians or quacks are already doing a brisk business in ritual cleansing, and doubtless the more enterprising stall-owners will try presenting a bill to the Palleseen Resident. Which will not in any way help intra-departmental tensions.

The Resident, Pallesand's diplomatic anchor in Bracinta, is a solid woman with more than a whiff of Aunt Ostrephy about her. Like Aunt Ostrephy, she is duly unimpressed. She spends fifteen minutes with Angilly up before her desk, pointing out that when she wrote to the Commission for a loan of additional staff she'd thought it implicit that said staff were possessed of a basic level of competence, rather than fresh out of the phal. And Angilly could point out the inadequacies of the standard brief, but the Resident outranks her and it wouldn't go well. Besides, the brief is only out of date on this point because, when it was drawn up, nobody in their right mind foresaw Outreach turning up with a demon. Exceptional Stratagems has been in existence for around seven years now, slowly expanding its remit, but it remains one of the least known – and certainly understood – branches of Correct Appreciation.

After which chewing out, Angilly retires to the taverna nearby the Resident's office with her team and considers how much she's starting to dislike Bracinta.

"She calls us in," she points out. "Oh so urgent, potential reversals, need some new faces. And she gets her new faces and straight away everything that goes wrong is on me." Covering with her bitching that it really is on her. Complacent, assuming it would all be in the brief. Everyone knows those things are put together by some antique clerk back on the Archipelago who hasn't ever been on a boat.

Benallers, arguably the chief cause of the mess, leans back in his chair and toasts her with his tin cup. "That," he said, "is what a promotion gets you. Nothing but hassle."

The other two members of her staff snicker dutifully, but Ben holds her gaze just a second and she feels a stab of guilt. Not her fault, again, but – also again – her responsibility. It isn't as though she furiously finagled to get a Fellow's rank badge but, after Lasaret took up that Sage's post on the Archipelago, *someone* was going to get to wear his boots. It might have been some outsider foisted on them, because she and Ben are both young for a Fellowship. But if it was to be one of them, then it might easily be the other. And, in the end, it had been her, not him.

He doesn't resent her for it. That isn't the point. The point is that they'd both lain awake wondering just why the cards fell that way. Is it her family – Aunt Ostrephy's influence at play maybe? Or is it the demon-taint, the creeping unsoundness of Benallers' specialist discipline impacting on his prospects? She can believe that.

Or is it the other thing?

"Is there anything else they didn't tell us, you think?" Sindler asks. *She's* come down instantly and immovably on the side of blaming the brief, as usual refusing to countenance that *her people* had done anything wrong. She's a kid, fresh out of the orphanage and without any influential aunts to help her along, but that's one of the reasons for the orphanages. Places that meant no-prospect no-parent gutter brats like Sindler get a phalanstery education and a rank badge and a chance to serve the Sway as something other than a footslogging trooper. Sindler is sharp and loyal and capable, and an early life of scrounging and petty theft taught her a lot of transferrable skills.

"Problem with this place," says Tinsly, their fourth, "is it's bloody *complicated*." Pronouncing the word as though it was a seven-generations curse from some heathen cult, because Tinsly has spent most of his long career marching on paper and he has a bureaucrat's loathing of people trying to make his job harder than it needs to be.

Bracinta is a crumbling old place these days, but rich still. Turmeric and dyes and cotton for half the uniforms across the Palleseen Sway, plus the locals have a couple of decanting techniques that Correct Erudition is still learning from, so the place produces a modest but steady flow of raw magic. About a decade ago they had a king, while also having a large number of relatives of the king who all thought they should be king, and things went about as well as that usually goes, with these barbaric political systems. A lot of important people died, the halls of the Wolf Palace ran red with blood, and then so did the streets of the capital. The heir vanished, probably into the river, and a consortium of viziers – whose backed horses had all fallen fatally at one fence or another – called in outside aid to stop the entire country descending into chaos. Some of that aid had come from the Loruthi, those canny merchant-adventurers who'd been gleefully parcelling up the known world with their Palleseen opposite numbers for a couple of decades now. The rest came from the Palleseen Sway, well known for their fairness, respect for the rule of law, and ability to put down any amount of rioting with a double line of batons stretched across one end of the street.

The upshot was that the Loruthi got their merchant factors settled in the rich southern plantations, with the turmeric and the wine and the places they farmed those weird walking fish. The Palleseen, meanwhile, received a standing invitation in the north of the country to maintain a staff of advisors, backed by a respectable garrison. Pal uniforms on the streets took over from the local militia as peacekeepers. Peace, therefore, had been kept, barring the occasional demon-induced hysteria. And the north is where the cotton farms are, and where the capital is, so the Pals can feel they've done very well out of the business. Except the north is also where the unrest is. The Hackle Throne of Bracinta sits empty, but the heir is allegedly still out there somewhere, and every so often some old-timer from the days of the last king starts making noises about how things were better back in the day.

"I mean, this ties our hands behind our back," Tinsly says, mostly to Ben. "I've got the papers on a whole search crew, loose-and-leave-'em lads. Don't reckon I get to use 'em now."

Benallers nods. They used the tactic in their last assignment: a clutch of low-grade demons just released over a wide area with some basic pattern-recognition instructions, and see what they report back with. It doesn't seem that Magnelei will react well to a plague of prying imps, though.

"If we were to try anything like it," he says thoughtfully, "then I think we'd need to contract for *simulacratia*."

Tinsly scowled. "*That*," he spits, "is altogether too much work. Even assuming the locals couldn't tell a *simula* straight off, no matter how human they looked. And they get uppity. They argue."

"That is part of the discipline," Benallers says mildly.

Tinsly's doing that thing where he disagrees with Ben – the senior demonist – while pretending to just talk to the air. "It don't have to be. Kings Below can kit you up with a dozen quick as you like, standard terms, so long as you don't get fancy with your requirements."

"Dross," says Ben derisively.

"Sometimes all you need is dross," Tinsly tells the air. "They're demons, not racehorses. The contract's all."

"That's like saying you can scrawl on a tableth in chalk, and it's still good enough for service. Fine, good, and then you rub off half the letters with your thumb and what've you got left? A baton that won't fire when you give the word," Benallers is still lounging, but he hasn't sipped at his cup for a while and Angilly knows him well enough to see the anger.

"It ain't, though," Tinsly says, still mild, still not-quite-engaging. "It's like them stamping the word in with a press so they can do a hundred in an hour, rather than some artificer taking ten minutes on each with a set of engraving tools. Forgive me for speaking out of turn, Magister, but you've seen the latest 'Cep-Strat manuals same as I have. Quantity's what they're after these days. Demons as bludgeon, not the scalpel work you're after. Demons as vanguard and line-breakers on the field." And at last he meets Ben's eyes, not without sympathy honestly. Just telling it the way it is. "Be happy. The department got what it was after ever since it was dreamed up by folks like you. It got taken seriously. It got fit into the tactical manuals. And just our good luck the Kings Below have whole camps full of cheap demons they can let us have, as many as we've got the papers for."

"This isn't conjuration, it's commerce," says Benallers.

"If only," Tinsly jibes. "Then we'd be with Correct Exchange and we could make some real money."

Ben drinks, ostentatiously casual, a man who doesn't care. And then decides he does care. "This is just shoddy workmanship," he tries. "Unworthy of us. There is an art we're neglecting, and who knows when we'll need it? The art of negotiation, conjurer to demon, over a precisely tailored service. A tool for all tasks, if one has the will and the wit to achieve it. Not this bulk commodity buying with the Kings. That's not how it is in Allor."

Tinsly looks awkward, breaking off his gaze again. He's a good decade older than Ben or Angilly and only a Cohort-Invigilator. Just a low-grade censor of prose until Exceptional Stratagems started recruiting, when it turned out he had just the right sort of twisty mind to oversee a good conjuration. And, with a Pal's pragmatism, he's very much of the new school of demonist who prefers the low-grade but reliable results of contracting with the Kings Below, rather than the bespoke arrangements Benallers had been taught.

"Magister, with respect," he says and, unlike most people who used the phrase, he actually means it, "I'd knock off that talk. I know it's your heritage and all, and where half our trade comes from, but the way the Allorwen talk of demons sounds mighty like religion to the wrong ears. You know they're rattling sabres on that side of the sea right now."

"Nobody's going to be invading Allor any time soon," Benallers says easily. "Telmark, on the other hand, is overdue a perfecting. That's what I hear." And Angilly can't tell whether he believes it or not.

★

Sindler is not a demonist, although she's proved admirably unfazed at having demons sporadically about the place. What she is, though, is a good fixer, and Angilly is already comfortable delegating that kind of work to her. Hence, the next morning finds them already expected by His Eminence Vesalreder, a balding, soft-looking man with a bony nose, one of the more prominent viziers in Magnelei. His prominence means that they meet him in the Wolf Palace, in a cushion-strewn antechamber just outside the throne room itself, with fountains and a beautifully crafted mechanical tree whose metal branches bear jewelled birds which break into snatches of melodic song at random intervals. Angilly initially finds it charming, exactly the sort of artifice that might be profitably imported into the Palleseen Sway. After the nineteenth time it bursts into life in the middle of someone's sentence she's ready to tear it up by its copper roots.

Northern Bracinta has a lot of viziers. They are the men – almost exclusively men – who invited the Pals in after the whole blood-in-the-streets succession struggle. Each one of them will tell you to your face that they're only awaiting the return of the true king, and in the interim they perform what poor services they can to keep Bracinta whole and prospering. Each one of them would, Angilly knew, have slit the throat of anyone turning up claiming descent from the royal line, and their vizierly robes of state hide a lot of capacious pockets that they busily stuff full the moment anyone lets them alone with the treasury. She reckons that at some point half the viziers will have a major falling out with the other half over who gets to pry the last jewelled fittings from the royal bedchamber, and then the Palleseen will get to cinch their noose that much tighter about the neck of Bracinta when someone comes begging for their intervention. And maybe then the place can be assigned a Perfector and be inducted formally into the Sway, and all these parasites can be thrown in the river to swim with the lost heir.

Right now, though, the Vizier Vesalreder is not concerned about his fellows, but about a mainstay of the old regime, one of the royalist loyalists nobody ever put a sword in. Or at least, according to rumour, they did but not hard enough.

"General Halseder," Vesalreder explains. "If indeed it is him at all. If indeed he is not dead and it is only his name like a banner they are using. His foxes only, we say they are."

And the vizier speaks good but imperfect Pel, and this is some Bracite figure of speech that doesn't come over properly. One of the talents that Sindler brings is a gift for quickly and superficially grasping new languages, though, and she goes back and forth with the man until she can explain. "The tail, he means. There's a saying, about the tail of the fox. They hold them up, so you look out in the fields and you see the tail, but… maybe the fox isn't there?"

Benallers points out that neither makes any sense nor is actually true about foxes, but apparently in Bracinta they have some magic foxes. And right now there's a lot of fox tails in the fields with General Halseder's colours tied to their ends, but Vesalreder doesn't believe the old warhorse is anywhere near the business. Just a convenient name from the old days for dissidents to rally to.

"They only now gather in strength," he points out, toying with the fantastically ornamented edging of his robe. "But an enemy they will seek out, so their voice it rings out across the city. To undo all the cords we have tied about our poor state, to keep back the anarchy, that is what they will seek. In the name of bringing back the old ways. Should they grow strong and bold, I fear for the safety of your uniforms on the streets of Magnelei."

It's a threat, in a way. The Pals have done very well after being invited in as peacekeepers. Vizierly pockets weren't the only ones being filled. But one upshot is that men like Vesalreder can hide behind the charcoal grey of the Palleseen soldiers when there's discontent being handed out. He and his fellows make sure that the Pal presence is the most public symbol of the current regime.

"Duly noted," Angilly tells him. "You think we should have a fox hunt, then."

"Obviously it is not for me to advise the advisors," says Vesalreder, examining his many rings. "A warning between friends, of poor weather sighted, this is. To say more would be to exceed the humility of my position."

Tinsly and Sindler are lodging with the Resident's staff, partly for space reasons and partly because they're well-placed to pick up on scuttlebutt. Angilly and Benallers, as Fellow- and Companion-Invigilator respectively, merit a guest room each, which are pokey and airless. Instead the pair of them repair to a private room in a nearby taverna to talk.

They go over the plan, the one still just coming together with a lot of gaps. Or at least Angilly goes over it, a game attempt to keep her work face on, until Ben's monosyllables and staring into his cup defeat her.

"Talk to me," she says, hand on his. "It's not the promotion, is it?"

He looks at her warily, and she feels a sudden stab at that distance between them. They've worked together for five-years-and-change, balanced the personal and the professional like tightrope walkers, but now everything is off-kilter. "I mean obviously it's the promotion," he says loudly, burlesquing outrage. "They laugh at me, they mock my talents! They dare defy the dread conjurer Benallers? I shall call up a thousand demons and conquer the Archipelago forthwith!"

And he's trying to make her laugh, and she does laugh, but doesn't feel it. Because even though it's a joke, an obvious joke, there are probably ears who, overhearing it, would be scrabbling to write a report about the half-Allorwen making threats. Being disloyal. Not, after all, one of us. *The real reason that it was my promotion*, she thinks. He can't read her mind, of course. Not even demons can. But somehow he knows and says, "You earned it. You're good. A Fellow at twenty-nine! Be proud of it. It's not that."

She wants to push it; to explore the edges of the real worry. The way the world is changing around him. The way his discipline has been taken out of his hands and turned into something transactional and profane. And has he never noticed that *profane* is exactly how the Pals like their magic? No reverence, no regalia, no complex rituals of respect for the infernal entities he entered into contracts with. Just Tinsly's forms in bulk, like ordering twenty pairs of boots from the stores.

She doesn't get to ask, because at that point the door slams open and a man muscles in, half a dozen others after him. Bracites in their open-fronted robes, bare chests, ornate belts, knives. The man in front should stand out because he's older, and because there's less of him, one arm ending at the elbow. Instead he stands out because he's so clearly in charge. His craggy face blazes with authority.

Angilly flicks a glance at Benallers. He has a hand to his belt – not for a knife but for contracts. A sudden influx of demon in an enclosed space is a risky emergency option, but sometimes you work with what you have.

She gives the savage-looking old man a bright look that contrives to ignore the way he has his hand on his knife-hilt. Below the table, her own adopts a similar pose, and she wonders what it would be like to go blade to blade with the man in this small room. To her surprise, some part of her supplies the prediction *Exhilarating*. It's been a while since she's had a really good one-on-one for decent stakes.

"General Halseder, I presume," she says pleasantly, and the old man scowls a confirmation.

The fox hunt starts late the next morning, and causes even more headaches for the Resident because, as well as commandeering three whole squads of soldiers, Tinsly and Benallers are out with everything they can contract for. At least a dozen separate demons of various unsightly shapes, hopping and lurching alongside Pal soldiers who don't like them much more than the locals do. Kicking in doors and shoving search warrants in people's faces. Rooting out old men and women who might still have some royalist flags hidden at the bottom of a closet. Causing a stink, basically. Stirring things up. So that either – as Angilly explains to the Resident and Vesalreder both – they'll flush out General Halseder, should there actually be a fox attached to the offending tail. Or alternatively the challenge to the old guard will be sufficient that Halseder will emerge from the woodwork to avoid losing face, whether or not he's anything to do with the whole unrest Vesalreder complained about. Or, as a third option, there'll not be hide nor hair of the fox to be seen, and his pointed absence will be a bucket of cold water on anyone trying to use his name to fan the flames of discontent. That's the plan.

The Resident has taken all of this relatively poorly, and her face promises that she'll ensure that all costs and consequences will find their way onto the permanent record of a certain newly-promoted Fellow-Invigilator of her acquaintance. Vesalreder, on the other hand, is positively eager. This sort of decisive, provocative action on the part of his Palleseen allies means he's going to get everything he wants, with all the blame falling on the foreigners. A situation with nothing but profit in it, leaving the whole city scowling at every uniform on the streets, and nobody looking over Vesalreder's shoulder as he nips into the treasury with some newly-empty pockets.

In the room beside the throne room – the one with the annoying tree – he entertains Angilly and Sindler lavishly as they awaited news.

"It is about time," he says, "that reminders were given to the loud voices in this city. Do they want another week of blood? Do they not remember how it was, before we brought them peace and stability?" He shakes his head ruefully. "They do not, for they were not there. They have only heard fool's stories of a golden time that never was."

The mechanical birds burst into a flourish of song just as he finishes speaking. He has the timing of the thing perfectly, fitting his words around its twittering, while Angilly constantly finds it treading on the ends of her sentences. Vesalreder isn't the only one who can use the artifice as a point of conversational emphasis, though. When the song dies away, General Halseder is standing in the room with them.

Vesalreder chokes, eyes bulging. He points a trembling finger at the one-armed old man with the knife, as though Angilly might have overlooked him amongst the room's lavish furnishing.

She pays a great deal of attention to the contents of her cup. Although she has brought her rapier as well as her knife to this meeting, just in case Halseder decides to go above and beyond his part of the deal.

He doesn't, in the end. In fact, he's neater and more discreet than she gave him credit for. He has people with him and they bundle Vesalreder into a sack. Halseder is an adherent of the absentee royal line, after all, and probably shedding blood within the Wolf Palace is poor form.

"Well?" she asks, once the people and the sack had gone.

Halseder stares at her for a long time, then nods and leaves. And that's the end of this particular round of Bracite unruliness. The fox pulls its tail back in. The locals settle down and allow peace to be kept. All for the price of one less venal vizier. And yes, the viziers are the faction the Pals made deals with, back after all those royal scions and their assassins had painted the palace red. But it's like Lasaret always said. Sometimes you had to play fast and loose with who you made happy. Vesalreder wanted to make the Pals his lightning rod for civic discontent, but there's a different solution for that equation and it relies on subtracting one particularly despised vizier from the maths. Not even a scapegoat, given how deep Vesalreder's pockets had been.

★

She regroups with her people shortly after, or that's the plan. And she'll remember it for a long time, perhaps all her life. Not just how things go wrong, but how the trouble seems to come from a clear sky, unheralded, just as they've sorted out all their problems and completed their assignment. She should be drafting her final report, commendations all round. Except…

Not as though the warning signs weren't there. Just that she contrived to ignore them. Made assumptions, just like with the brief.

It's just Tinsly and Sindler, when she gets to the taverna. Where's Benallers, she asks. Is he getting the drinks in or…?

They look at her owlishly. "Wasn't he with you?" Sindler says.

Halseder betrayed us, she decides instantly. Or else some demon-hating local had kept a knife sharp for the man. Or else…

She's up and running for the Residency immediately. Filing a request for search parties, all patrols to search for Companion-Invigilator gone missing in the course of his duty. Distinguishing features? The man who was with me just last time I was here. The demonist. Not the old man, the other one, the half-Allor.

That's when she begins to find out the full shape of how it's all gone wrong. Of how she'd only seen the tail, after all, and not the whole of the fox. Because there is a weird unwillingness about the Residency staff to actually admit that she ever had a half-Allor demonist on her staff. To consent to the fact of Benallers' existence at all. And the more she asks, the more blank looks she gets, and she's been in uniform enough to know when people know absolutely what you're talking about but won't admit it. And, because

Outreach doesn't deal in hammering rank badges on desks and making demands, she retreats from their barefacery and gathers her people.

She has all sorts of plans, then. About going head to head with the Resident. About going rogue in the city. About finding General Halseder and making some sort of common cause. All these plans in the hour she's given before the news reaches her. That, over on the other side of the sea, the Palleseen army has marched into Allor. The filthy demon-worshippers had been asking for it, with their vile practices. If ever there was a nation that offended the notion of perfection it was surely Allor.

And her people retreat from her, either to give her space or in case she's about to do something career-endingly rash. They cede the table to her and she sits there, in the corner of a Bracite taverna, and tries to work out whether he ducked out ahead of Correct Speech, or whether they got him. And over the next few years she'll make what tacit inquiries she can, to feel out the truth, but she will never, ever know.

The Usmai Situation

He left a hole in her, when she found him gone. When they took him. And she uses every channel, pushes her luck right to the very point where some higher power would slap her down, and *still* it isn't enough to find out what happened to Companion-Invigilator Benallers. Whether he ended his days in the hands of Correct Speech, or died in his mother's homeland fighting his father's people, or fled to the ends of the world to avoid being ground between those opposing teeth, or… She doesn't know. She will never know. The world keeps its secrets. Only the hole is left.

It should be the thing that breaks her. Or perhaps opens her eyes, some dread revelation about the powers she serves and the job she does. Except, is it anything she didn't know, and is the alternative so grand? By then, she's seen enough venal viziers and murderous priests and barbarous, imperfect places to understand why the Palleseen Commission must exist. And to accept that the perfection, when it comes, will be worth it. On average, in aggregate, according to utilitarian calculations. In the interim, every department of the Sway does its best, one eye on what is to come, but the other firmly on what *is*. And Outreach most of all, the department that goes in ahead of the armies. Living the Rain Life, making the best of it in lands where the light of perfection is barely more than a guttering candle on a hillside a hundred miles away.

She doesn't break. No revelations drop. But something changes, nonetheless. Ask *Why?* of the Angilly who went into Bracinta and probably her answer – the true one she wouldn't have told you – would have included some nod to ideology, the overriding *rightness* of things they'd taught her in the phal. The stiff principles she still had despite the flexibility that Outreach work demanded. And if there is a casualty to Benallers' vanishing – other than Benallers – it is that. Ask her *Why?* now and the answer she won't tell you has a great deal more to do with what Angilly wants for Angilly. Her ambitions for herself, that will serve the cause of perfection because it's perfection handing out the rewards and promotions. A grey death of the moral soul, stripping away her hierarchy of things until only the self is left. A condition she sees on the faces of half the officers she associates with. The older half, in general.

In the three years since Bracinta she worked four more assignments, each more complex than the last. Reporting to Residents or Perfectors, but very much on her own recognizance. Discovering that the loss of that last measure of rigidity is, professionally, only a convenience. She goes to lands where the Palleseen presence is not measured in boots and batons but in merchants, adventurers and spies. She meets with petty royalty and clan chiefs whose eminence the Pals might nudge along in return for concessions. She meets with philosophers and ideologues whose causes are so riddled with context she can barely understand them, but whose burning need to either overthrow or shore up the current social order is something that might serve the Sway. In Cazarkand she sits across a table from a suave, funny man who worships a chthonic serpent god that's supposed to eat hearts. She's aware that she likes him a great deal, his wit and his ability to laugh at himself and his god and still believe in both, and that is a betrayal of her Palleseen upbringing. Simultaneously, no matter what arrangements they come to here and now, at some point her compatriots will break his temple doors, cast down his idols and destroy his faith, and that is a betrayal of every word she is saying to him. She holds both betrayals in her head and feels no tug of contradiction. It's all part of the game. The point is to win.

After the Cazarkand job she gets called back to the Archipelago. Not always a happy moment, but she knows she's done well, and not crossed anyone senior, so she permits herself some modest expectations.

Professor-Invigilator Flockersly has been running Outreach since there was an Outreach, the diplomatic wing of the Palleseen Sway having had to run to catch up with its military endeavours. Or, probably that's not true. He's old but not *that* old. Still, the department has expanded dramatically under his governance, as he progressed from a slender young man with a mind like a corkscrew to this weighty hulk of an old one with a mind like a whole Inquirer's toolkit of clamps, probes and needles.

He is probably aware, she guesses, that outside his office people refer to him as 'Flossy'. It breeds complacence that he can use against his interdepartmental rivals.

Flockersly – and she doesn't make the mistake of thinking of him by that undignified nickname because complacence is something she cannot afford – is a massive, decaying figure, chins and jowls and a pinkish complexion, buttons straining at every join of his jacket and the bottom three popped undone despite the best efforts of his aide every morning. He has exquisite tea in exquisite little cups, and a plate of honeyed cakes prepared by an Oloumanni chef to a recipe otherwise extinct in the world following the destruction of a culinarily-blessed religion. Flockersly oversaw that destruction during the liberation of Oloumann from its plague of incestuous gods. Flockersly brought conjuration into Correct Appreciation's remit after the industrial and military application of demons proved severable from superstition and ritual. Flockersly has watched the Palleseen Sway grow like his own waistline, both of which expansions of territory he can claim significant credit for. Being across his enormous desk from him is the first time Angilly has ever been in the presence of someone who actually sits on the Temporary Commission of Ends and Means that steers the fate of Pallesand.

She's properly honoured, obviously, but more interested in what's in it for her. She's thirty-two and a Fellow. It's an audience more august than she'd looked for.

"The Usmai situation," says Flockersly, "is complicated."

She nods. She read the dossier on the boat.

"Been in our sights for years, obviously. Decades really. All the states down that ways. Made some progress in the region." He slurps his tea, coarse as a costermonger. Smacks his lips. Dares her to wince. "Not in Usmai itself, though. Thought we'd got our shot back when the old Alkhand died. Nice little succession struggle brewing, brother against brother. But the Resident at the time dropped the ball, and we were shut out of it. Complicated. Too much history. Too many spoons in the pot."

His eyes – narrow, pressed half-shut by the flesh of his

face, gleaming sharp with intellect – fix on her. She sips the tea, which is so good that, if she hadn't already been determined to win herself an office like this, it would have lit the fires of ambition in her by its quality alone.

"Your record is full of questionable choices," he tells her.

She sips the tea again. Very pointedly doesn't freeze or stare or protest, because those are signs of insecurity and guilt. The dossier had intimated she might be sent to Usmai to support the current Resident's efforts on behalf of the Sway. The dossier had not suggested that this was going to be one of *those* meetings. But the problem with Outreach is that *your* business-as-usual is any other department's arrested-on-charges-of-unsound-conduct and so you can never honestly say *I've done nothing wrong* because, from a certain rigid point of view, you always had.

If Correct Appreciation have decided to clean house, it seems a great deal of trouble to go to, to ship her all the way to the office of this important man, rather than just to have Correct Speech bundle her off like maybe they did with Benallers. But who is she to teach the Commission its job?

"Hunting accident, they tell me," Flockersly says. He's not the first senior officer who talks like this. Just giving her the abbreviated notes of the conversation they're having, leaving her to fill in the gaps from the knowledge she's apparently supposed to have.

One hand like a puffy pink paw slides a paper towards her across the expanse of the desk. The onion-skin stuff the administration uses for orders and dispatches because it's remarkably hard for forgers to play games with.

An eye-flick at the handful of carefully-written lines there, parsing the surface layer of meaning for anything encoded by force of habit. "Ah," she says. "A hunting accident, or a 'hunting accident', Magister?"

Flockersly chuckles, a liquid sound like bad plumbing. "Honestly, most likely the former. It's one of those places where the nobs like their sports, and the wildlife can be overly bracing."

Her eyes catch the words *Tiger-Crab*, and she has no context whatsoever for them. *A* crab, *seriously?* It hardly seemed a dignified way for the Palleseen Resident in Usmai to die.

"Bracinta," says Flockersly. "Cazarkand. Lemas. The Holy Regalate of Stouk. Jarokir." And a particular turn to that last place-name that tells her, somehow, that it was a test. Sending her there, to the very place that consumed her family and seared her childhood from her. That they'd been watching her even back then.

Or that Flockersly wanted her to believe it, anyway. Twisty old bastard that he was.

"Magister," she said. The word alone, respect without risk, no opinion ventured.

"A lot of questionable decisions for someone so young," he said ponderously. His aide arrived, topped up their cups and brought a second plate of even more elaborate-looking cakes she wasn't going to touch.

"Magister," she neither agreed nor disputed.

"Your predecessor," a jab at the paper to indicate he of the crab-related fatality, "was conventional."

She sips her tea. Her professional *sangfroid* is noted.

"The Loruthi are all over that part of the world. Clever people," Flockersly says. "Open the door a crack, they're already in by the window. You know."

"Magister," she agreed.

"There's a gallete heading to our people in Peor, just next door. Departs tomorrow. Be on it. Brief's in your temporary quarters," says the great man. That many disconnected sentences in a single utterance seem to exhaust him. A flap of thick fingers indicates she can leave him to investigate the cakes on his own. At the door, though, his voice lifts to arrest her.

"You can carry yourself in a fight, can't you, Sage-Invigilator?"

The first words eclipse the last, taking her all the way back to the star-shaped piste at the orphanage, her useless but envied skill that she has, since, maintained for no other reason than she enjoys it and is very good at it. Except right then she has an almost mystical sense that, somehow, her lifelong application to the duel was all because somehow she knew she'd be here at this moment, hearing those words from him. "Yes, Magister," she says, and only registers the rest of what he said when she's sitting in her temporary quarters with the promotion papers and the Sage's badge in her hands.

The Cleansing

"You cannot move for skulls, round here." Sage-Invigilator Palinet, Palleseen Resident in Peor, is a fussy little woman with a mop of dark curls and a hand of jointed brass and wood. It has a tableth set in its back, and closes about her teacup with a click. The tea at the Residence is not of Flockersly's standard, spiked with a bitter tonic Palinet says is the best defence against this season's swamp fevers. Swamps are the other things you couldn't move for, in Peor.

"I mean the actual *Empire* is literally dead. Closed its doors, the whole capital city a living tomb. I went there once," Palinet goes on. "Very impressive if you like closed doors. But it's been an age, and the *idea* of the place still has its hooks in all the Successor States." Meaning the collection of nations that were formerly tributaries to the Moeribandi Empire, but have been charting their own destinies for centuries. Places like Peor and Usmai and a half-dozen others on both sides of the Garmoer range.

Bracinta was hot, and Farasland was cold, but what the Successor Coast is, is *humid*. Angilly understands that it takes most Pals a month before they can actually go about their business without wilting. Most Pals didn't spend years in Jarokir with its rains, though. Not quite a memory of childhood, more like someone had tried to draw a picture of it from her descriptions. She's bearing up far better than anyone else, though. The rest who disembarked from the gallete are fanning themselves and slumping in their seats, and the Fellow-Broker she played cards with on the journey has already gone to sleep.

Palinet has a scarf about her neck, incredibly, save that a servant hurries over at her gesture to dash it with cooled, scented water from the cellars. That's how the Peosts do it, apparently, when even their own climate becomes too much for them.

"We've made solid inroads here," Palinet explains. "Ten years back there was a big throw down with Goshumai. Peosts were getting their arses whipped. Begged us on their knees to come lend a hand. Now we've got garrisons in half the towns, our advisors tell the new kid what laws to pass and our goods don't get taxed at the ports." Measuring Angilly with her gaze, one Resident to another. Partly a boast, partly a roadmap. "But Usmai's the plum. Peor's just the poor relation." A look that took in how young Angilly was for the post, not necessarily judging, but noting the fact down in case anyone came round later asking, *Where did we go so wrong?*

Usmai, the big dog in the region, the dominant power the others all watched. Angilly's problem. Her opportunity.

"It's the family," Palinet says. "Or that's what my people tell me. You know how it is. You can have too much of a good thing, with royals. With heirs. That's how this region's always gone. Some state has a Big Man with a good grasp of fundamentals, wins some fights, exacts some tribute, then he has too many kids, and the succession screws everything up and it all falls over. Then it's someone else's turn."

Two days later Angilly's on a boat, a coastal trader,

swapping stories with a merchant factor while she watches for the mouth of the Osio, that marks the boundary between Peor and Usmai.

The music drifts out to them as the coaster tacks past the sea wall. Angilly's first sight of the port city of Alkhalend is the tangled maze of the docks. Piers and boats, rafts and floating houses, lashed together in a chaotic mess that makes a whole town in itself. And then her eyes lead her up. Past the warehouses and factoras, beyond the great heaped mound where meaner housing are stacked one atop the other in an ant's hill of slanted roofs and flimsy walls and makeshift cane buttresses. Up the stepped pools that are the heart of the city, a waterfall cascading from on high in measured stages, each of which catches the morning light in a dance of rainbows. An upper city of grand stone palaces and gleaming gardens that clings to cliffs sculpted by time and water and the genius of architects. The silver and gold of the eaves, and of the roofs themselves, more mother of pearl than all the molluscs of the world could yield, sculpted in scalloped curves so that, when it rains, the entire upper city must glitter in a constant storm of falling spray.

And the whole city, turned out to welcome her.

Or not that, not at all, but turned out. The streets below thronging, every deck and jetty in the maze of docks populated. The true design of the city revealed: that what goes on at its heart can be witnessed by all, be they never so mean, be they never so lofty. The staggered pools of rainbow water halfway down the cliff, and the great arched cave cut into the rock, and the celebrants. The music from their pipes, their drumming and chanting, their high sad voices crying out at the vault of the heavens and Angilly says, "What the hell are they about?"

The merchant factor, who spent the voyage explaining that literally nobody knows the Successor Coast better than he does, shakes his head. "I have not the first bloody idea," he says. "They don't do this nonsense in Peor." As though Peor, because it boasted a few Pal garrisons, was now the benchmark for sanity.

"God stuff?" Angilly asked, and obviously it was god stuff, except: "I thought it was all skulls and dirges and tombs, this Dead Empire business?"

"Oh there's that, all over," the factor confirms, still boggling. "But all these places, they've got their own gods too. Peor, there's about nine of them, each one stupider than the last."

"And Usmai?"

"Some sort of frog I think?"

She stares at the cave mouth, which has been carved with something too fine in detail to be made out at this distance. Some sort of frog fails to emerge. The singing and music build slowly, with the implication it'll be a while.

The crowded network of docks will take all day to wind through, and doubtless there are customs and taxmen and possibly brigands and frog cultists. She suddenly decides she doesn't have time for that, because something very important is plainly going on, and as the new Palleseen Resident in Alkhalend she needs to know what.

"Have the ship's boat put out with a man to row me," she says. By the time it's ready she's back from her quarters with her rapier at her belt and a soldier's kitbag over her shoulder like she's no more than a trooper off on leave.

In Peor it had been oppressively hot. Stepping out where the final tier of waterfalls meet the sea, it's merely hot. The glittering haze of water cast up by the constant downward flow saturates the uniform jacket she's buttoned back, and the shirt beneath it. Her hair is already drooping out of the neat bun she pinned it into that morning. There is no time to stop for a change of clothes and a coiffeur. She finds a path that leads up, and even as she starts to ascend she hears the music change pitch, the voices wail in a new key, expectant, mournful, numinous. *A funeral*, she decides. *A sacrifice*. But those were commonplace things in ignorant, god-ridden countries. If a death, past or imminent, was on the cards, it was the death of kings. Of *Alkhands*, that being the appropriate Usmiat title.

There are people gathered at various stages up the cliffs, most of them looking priestly – how could one place have so many religious types exactly? A lot of them cast unfriendly looks her way, but she keeps going, and there are enough people in the local civilian dress, the drapey shawls and ornamented vests and loose trousers, that she doesn't feel she's intruded into some open-air sanctum sanctorum. Unless they're all priests in mufti.

Three levels further up she sees what's going on, although she doesn't understand.

A woman is standing in the middle of one of the pools. A dignified older woman, forty, maybe fifty. Hard to tell because Angilly isn't used to Usmiat faces yet. She wears a loose shawl and a long robe, already sodden at the hem. An ornate necklace of jade and topaz and amber hangs heavy about her neck. It is a thing of interlocking spirals and whorls that nonetheless suggests the spreading branches of a tree. Magnificent, exquisite in its craftsmanship, the sort of thing that would buy a good house back on the Archipelago.

There are priests nearby, mostly the heavyset jolly-aunt-and-uncle sort, although in her experience that doesn't mean the knives aren't going to come out. There's a very richly clad group of people at the pool's edge, watching. Far more ornamented than the regular more dispersed cloud of people who are still extremely richly dressed. She begins fumbling at her jacket buttons, getting them in the right holes, making herself at least borderline presentable.

She has read descriptions, from the Resident's aide she hasn't met yet. She cross-references the memory of them with what she can see of the most splendid of the onlookers. It's the old man's eyes that give them away, because during the struggle over who got to sit on the throne, he was blinded by his brother. The greenstone-plated skull in his hands, its eyes stoppered up with gems, is probably the former property of that brother. This, then, is the Alkhand of Usmai, and so the young man and the boy and the girl are presumably at least some of the children of the Alkhand of Usmai. And the woman in the pool…

There is a great deal of endurance and suffering in the lines of her face, and patience and nobility and the fact that none of these is infinite, and that sometimes burdens are best left behind.

She kneels down and unbinds her hair, twisting a serpentine silver cord out from heavy tresses until they fall past her shoulders and trail in the clear, still water. Angilly sees fish there, salamanders, water boatmen. Frogs, though none pretending to divinity.

The woman bends low, until the waters kiss her forehead. Angilly braces herself for the priest with the knife, knowing that there is nothing she can do. Indeed that, for diplomatic reasons, she'll probably have to nod and applaud politely as the water runs red all the way down to the harbour. But it's not that kind of ritual, apparently.

Two other priests are stepping forwards, thinner, with simpler and more encompassing robes, rather than the jolly-aunts-and-uncles who are showing a lot of bare skin down to their navels. Masked, these new ones. Eyeless, daubed with bright colours in stripes and patches. They raise the woman up and press just such a mask into her hands. When she dons it, she is one of them. Angilly can't quite say how she knows it. The woman is no longer herself. She is another person. She leaves with her two fellow masquers and it is weirdly difficult to tell which one of them is her, and which are the original priests.

The singing and the instruments reach a peculiar wailing that speaks of a universal loss. Hearing it, Angilly thinks of her parents, of Benallers. That is how she knows, for the first time, that she has given up on him still being alive. You could not hear that music and hold a living face in your mind, only the dead.

"And so it is," says a voice from behind her, in smooth but accented Pel, "that the Blessed Kaleithi severs herself from the side of His Tranquillity, the Alkhand Oparan, dissolving their bonds of thirty years and taking on the mantle of the Alborandi." Not an Usmiat accent, but one she knows.

He is a short man with long hands never still. He wears a bastard hybrid costume: an Usmiat shawl over his shoulders, but the long vest is bottle green and festooned with medals and braid, all the decoration that the Loruthi love to give themselves. He has a magnificent forked beard, oiled and curled and threaded with gold beads in the shape of bees.

"You must be my opposite number," he says, and makes an elegant, foreign obeisance. "The Bashonin Tarcomir, official emissary of the great nation of Lor. I'd say 'at your service' but we both know that would be a scurrilous piece of mendacity."

"Sage-Invigilator Angilly, Outreach Department," she tells him. She burns to know precisely what the hell was just going on with the woman and the water and the masks. The singing has stopped now, anyway, and everyone is rather ponderously leaving, with expressions of constipated solemnity. The older man, the Alkhand, lord of life and death across all Usmai, weeps stone tears from his stone eyes.

She cannot, of course, ask Tarcomir. Not yet at any rate. Not until she's established herself and has something to trade, or else she's indebting herself to the representative of a competing power. Although there is something about the way he stands, and the spark in his eye, that suggests she might actually quite enjoy getting to know him, once that is permissible.

Then there's a young man at her elbow, in a Pal uniform so rigidly perfect that he might be some kind of wooden mannikin and the heat bedamned. He takes her arm, nods pleasantly at the Bashonin Tarcomir, and very hurriedly gets her out of reach of anyone she might make a fool of herself in front of. Her aide has finally tracked her down.

The Ways of the Duel

You can carry yourself in a fight, can't you? was the question she'd been asked, when she'd been given this post. And it turns out she can't.

The air rings with the clash of blades. The spectacular clash, in fact; absurdly dramatic. Not the tight little click and clatter of rapiers, but the ringing of curved edges off one another, bright and fierce like lightning on the ear, punctuated with the grunts and gasps and little barks of triumph of the fighters. This is *clavamachy*, the meeting of the curved hacking swords they call *clavars*. One half of Usmai's ancient duelling tradition, that is an essential part of any high-class Usmiat's education. Specifically, the half that includes men.

The Alkhand is a man. That's how it is. Unlike a lot of imperfect nations, Usmai doesn't subjugate one gender or the other, robbing itself of half its native potential in order to uphold some antique and inequitable privilege. There are, however, things men do, and things women do, and one of the things men do is rule.

The Alkhand, that stone-eyed old man with his brother's skull as a keepsake, sired four still-living children on the woman who would later walk into the pools, and out of his life. Three of them are boys – men, now – and one of those will be Alkhand in time. Meaning that a major part of

Angilly's role here will be to ensure that the incoming regent smiles upon the fortunes of Pallesand and its perfection.

There's only one pair of duellists fighting, now. Everyone else has stopped to watch, from respect. And also because both combatants are rather good.

If she was called upon to picture a warrior prince, then Angilly would – well, probably she'd instinctively imagine someone more Pal in complexion and features, because that's how imagination works most of the time. But that would have been before she met Gorbudan, eldest son of the Alkhand of Usmai and heir presumptive. Not heir because he's oldest. Refusing to shackle themselves to primogeniture in Usmai has pros and cons, as the current Alkhand's brother's skull could tell you. Heir presumptive because of everything else about him. Gorbudan has a long, lean face with a fierce beard, his unbound hair night-black and whirling free about his bared shoulders. The familial high forehead, hawkish brows and nose. A man made for telling his troops to take the trench or wall or hill in a manner that would have them scrambling from cover joyously to do his will. A man made to lead them, sword in one hand and baton in the other. Not the greatest courtier, perhaps, and he's already had a couple of throwdowns with his father, periods of exile at his fortress of Mantekor, exhibitions of rash pride. But he's the man who will be Alkhand and everyone knows it. He gets away with a lot.

Angilly has been introduced. His stare, below those raptorial brows, weighed her up and saw One More *Kepishi*, the word they used for the visiting powers from across the ocean. And she turned on the charm, and she secured this invitation to watch the heir flourish his steel – she'd had to check with her aide, Storry, to ensure it wasn't some double-entendre because her Usmiri is still a bit short on subtext. She'd buckled on her rapier and shoved a clean shirt in her belt-satchel and assumed she'd get to show Gorbudan just what she could do.

In Usmai, the long straight duelling sword is the *skia*, and it's the province of women. Which obviously works well for Angilly, the woman, on one level. But something that the previous Resident's notes did not at any point mention was that one does *not* mix clavamachy and skiamachy. Men cannot duel women, and vice versa. It isn't done.

And Angilly has had several noblewomen invite her to their sand circles, and has acquitted herself admirably, upheld the honour of the phalanstery and the Palleseen Sway. Polite applause from Storry and that pleasant humming the Usmiat do, to express approval. But none of the women she has impressed is going to be Alkhand. And Gorbudan is. Gorbudan, who loves to fight, and is at this moment deep in clavamachy with Tarcomir, the Loruthi delegate.

Of course Tarcomir was always going to be ahead of her. He's been in his post six years and she's been here barely a month. But the heir loves hunting, and he loves games of strategy, but of all things he loves duelling, and that was where she was supposed to shine.

Honestly, she should write to Flockersly and explain why she can't properly fulfil her brief. They should trawl Outreach's roster to find some up-and-comer who has a good record and a quick sword and, most importantly, a pair of testicles. Except that would be an admission of inadequacy, for all it's over something that was decided before she left her mother's womb. And it's not just about the advancement of the Sway. It's about *her*. This was to have been her big chance.

The duellists break. Tarcomir is holding his arm, his clavar on the ground, his hand up to concede the hit. The hum of approval swells. Angilly and Storry applaud so very politely.

She is not going to write home confessing her lack. She is going to find a way round this. She will practise the local games of strategy. She will hunt every species in the vicinity to extinction. Something.

Later, the Alkhand-presumptive leaves, laughing with Tarcomir, and most of the others, fighters and spectators both, also go because they were there to be seen by him. And probably Angilly should go with them and dance attendance but she isn't feeling overly diplomatic right now.

"Get a sword," she tells Storry.

His face is all-over panic. For a Resident's aide he has risibly little control over his features.

"Not one of those cleavers," she adds, when he goes for a clavar – the Usmiri word is the root of the Pel, "A rapier."

"Magister, we both know that's entirely inappropriate," he tries.

"We are not bound by these ridiculous customs."

He rolls his eyes at the couple of low-tier nobles facing off against one another across the vaulted, pearl-ceilinged hall. Under Angilly's unyielding gaze he picks up a skia and holds it entirely the wrong way. The local blades have a nasty hooked claw for a pommel, used in a variety of wicked little close-up manoeuvres. Even blunted for practice, Angilly still has the scratch of one across her upper arm. If Storry went for her the way he's doing, he'd end up impaling his own elbow.

"I take it this wasn't part of your curriculum at the phal," she notes.

"Magister, alas, it was not." She's learned that he's an extremely capable clerk and administrator. This was probably too much to hope for.

She looks around in case there's an Usmiat noblewoman she can work out her frustrations on. Earlier, in fact, she saw the sole princess of Usmai, youngest of the Alkhand's brood, up in the gallery. The girl's gone, though, and anyway she's only thirteen and isn't going to be inheriting anything of much except marriage to some useful ally.

Storry makes an apologetic shrug that has the hook of his pommel tear a rip in his shirt. He goes to put it back on the rack and someone takes it off him. Smoothly enough that, had it been sharp and had murder been in the offing, Storry would be very dead.

"Might I cross swords with you?" says the new man. Very definitely a man, holding a woman's blade and amazingly his balls haven't dropped off or his beard fallen out. And he's a local, not some expat looking to curry favour with the new Resident. A good-looking man, though a little baby-faced for her tastes. Not the hawkish fierceness of Gorbudan but enough Usmai nobility in his face to show some relation.

It's Storry who cues her. Not his place to just blurt things out in refined company but he tells her by his expression that this man is known to him, and is important.

"Sier," she says carefully, addressing him as a respected superior because that seems safest, "if you are sure." And what she *should* do is demure, evade, not permit him to humiliate himself. But right now she really wants to fight someone.

He holds the skia well, but not like an Usmiat woman would. Adjusting for that hook, but keeping his body in line, hand up and away rather than behind the back. A stance that's close cousin to her own Palleseen poise.

She tries a few exploratory passes. He is... adequate. The word still brings back memories of Aunt Ostrephy. Her aunt would not have approved of this man's fencing, but at least he's got the basics down, and a few tricks that she will have to add to her own repertoire. A weird bastard of styles, and a genuinely fun switch from right to left hand that gives him his single touch on her and makes her grin.

By then she's touched him four times – enough to show she's clearly better, but he's made her work for it and that's flushed a lot of the frustration out of her. She indicates the sand with the blunted tip of her weapon, a pose that allows her to offer a cessation while also letting her bring her blade into guard if her opponent has other ideas. He nods, sheened with sweat, instantly stripping off his ornate vest so that a servant can hurry over with a clean one. His body, thus glimpsed, is not the lean muscle Gorbudan probably possesses. *Probably*, given the crown prince didn't change before walking off laughing with the Loruthi ambassador. Her opponent is a little soft. *Not a soldier but a poet*, she thinks, and isn't immediately sure why. Then hearing the words again in Benallers' voice, his defensive counter when she teased him over the gut he was developing.

Storry stands in exactly the right place and holds up her clean shirt the right way so that she doesn't offer up any parts of the Palleseen negotiating position that aren't supposed to be on the table. When she's changed, and her aide has dashed cool scented water about her shoulders, neck and hair to cool her down and mask the sweat, her opponent is looking at her. Not with barbaric lust. Not with foreign hauteur. Not with a losing duellist's wounded pride. Calculatingly, in fact.

"Will you honour me with your company as I walk, Resident?" he asks. A very polite-formal way of putting it in Usmiri, and using her Pal title because she doesn't fit any of the local categories of address that wouldn't also be a covert insult.

She steals a look at the open book of Storry's face, which says *Yes*. On which basis, of course, she'd be delighted.

Outside the hall, in the water-misted air of the Constellar Gardens, they wind their way between the glittering of radiant flowers.

"Sier, may I ask who trained you?" she ventures. Probably he should speak first but her foreign-ness gives her licence.

He gives a quick little yap of laughter. "So that you might write to them with complaints?"

"Sier fights admirably." And the words are close in Usmiri and she very nearly said *adequately* despite everything.

"It is not first among my studies," he says, and then, "which were at the Killinbraan Nautical Institute, if you know it."

Killinbraan. A knot of islands untouched by humans for the whole history of the world, until they were discovered almost simultaneously by Palleseen and Loruthi mariners two generations ago. And now the site of a thriving township serving as the resupply point for half the civilized world's cross-oceanic shipping. A fishing port, a shipyard, a mercantile meeting point. And magic, as with most sudden centres of wealth and human activity. They scrape it off the rocks with the bird guano, she's heard. But as the potential of the place attracted the wealthy and powerful from Lor and Pallesand both, they built an odd little society with a lot of home conveniences. Including a renowned educational institution, half Palleseen phal, half Loruthi university. The Nautical Institute, noteworthy and cosmopolitan enough that the ambitious of many nations send their spare children there.

He looks at her. Even speaking to her, his attention was on the middle distance, a particular pensive look Usmiat cultivate, to show their minds are on higher things. When he turns his head, then, she knows it's performative, important.

"I have a gift to beg from you. I am not too proud," he says. And he'd fought her with a woman's sword in his hand. Because he was trained by foreigners, but also because he's *not* too proud, it seems.

She isn't quite sure how to play this, and Storry is too many steps behind along with a handful of the man's servants. She falls back on improvisation. "What might the Palleseen Sway do for you, Sier?" she asks, reads the reaction about the skin of his eyes, and adds, "Or I, Sage-Invigilator Angilly, as myself."

"The day you came to Alkhalend, you saw a ritual," he tells her frankly. "And I have heard the story of it from everyone in my family and everyone in the House of Tranquillity, and they tell it like a story ten generations old. But you are a foreigner. You are a *Kepishi*, they say, and the *Kepishi* have no manners and are arrogant and rude and do not know the proper way to go about anything."

She waits, stony faced.

"I need someone to tell me of it who is rude and has no manners and will not just say the words one is supposed to say," he tells her, earnest to the point of indecorum himself. "They say you saw my mother enter the pools and take the mask. Please. I was not there. I was aboard ship still. Tell me how it was."

This is how Angilly meets Dekamran, prince of Usmai, the second son.

The Broken Mirror

Three years on and she's mostly resigned herself to failure. Eventually. One of those curious situations where she knows her future holds an absolutely disastrous report home: an admission; a confession. But until then she can keep dictating her bright little missives to Storry and Outreach's solid headquarters back on the Archipelago doesn't need to know that it'll all collapse. She's done her bit, after all. Interceded for Pal merchants whose goods have been impounded or unfairly taxed; hosted a Pal poet and a musician to reasonable crowds, though to be honest cultural exports are not what Pallesand is really known for. She's tracked down a renegade trying to go to ground on her turf and handed him over to Correct Speech. She's liaised with her counterpart in Peor, whose own reports home are of a decidedly more cheery bent because that nation is well and truly on its way to a formal liberation, under Pal control in everything but formal name and the arse on the throne no more than a pampered figurehead. And she frowns at the wording of her thought, because who'd have an arse as a figurehead. The Peosts, apparently.

And she's been cultivating Dekamran, just in case Warrior Prince Gorbudan falls ill or something, although the man's health appears to be disgustingly robust. He has just returned from a hunt, in fact. A month-long hunt that was also a good excuse not to be under his father's feet for a while because Gorbudan is thrusting and energetic and wants more of a role in foreign policy than the Alkhand will devolve to him just yet. And the old man with the stone eyes is more and more cautious and withdrawn each year. Usmai is the muscular one amongst the Successor States this side of the mountains, and yet it won't flex, and so Gorbudan argues with his father, mostly in private but sometimes openly. And so he went hunting, to let things cool, but now he's back. Unlike Dekamran he always arrives at the right time, not because he's sly or mendacious but because he's basically a hero out of the mythic tales and therefore is always exactly where he's needed. Gorbudan the warrior prince, a man whose worst vices are the dreamed-of virtues of other men.

Angilly has decided she hates him. And it's mostly because when Gorbudan is in the capital he spends his time with Tarcomir of Lor as much as anyone, who has adroitly edged out all chance of Palleseen influence. Should that not mean she hates Tarcomir? The problems there are twofold. Firstly, when Gorbudan *isn't* around, Tarcomir is her opposite number, her peer, the man whose company she's so often in because, when national interests don't actively clash, she and he have a great deal in common. Secondly he's really good company. She can see why Gorbudan likes having the man around. Behind that absurdly glorious beard is an entertaining raconteur, a nimble dancer and actually a relatively decent man for a Loruthi and a diplomat. It makes a lot of sense for the two of them to just get together and share a drink because that's a much lower-stakes way of sorting things out than having a spat before the Alkhand.

Like Jarokir, of fond and unfond memory, Usmai has a rainy season. It would actually be the best time to see Alkhalend, if it wasn't for all the rain, because the waterfall that forms the city's centrepiece doubles in volume, a spectacular roaring torrent that fills the air across the entire bay with glittering spray. They call it *Orundama*, 'Thunder Month', even though it lasts almost three months, but that's why foreign calendars are all in need of Pal perfection honestly.

Thunder Month has been and gone, in which time the Alkhand has not left the House of Tranquillity, his palace. Not to hear the rain turn the pools of his gardens to broken mirrors. Not to hear the drops batter the last guttering blooms from the bushes. Not to wave his fractious eldest off hunting. Not for any reason. But today he is outside, the first clear day in a hundred. Today he has gathered his robes about him, his regalia, the White Petal Crown and the greenstone-plated skull of his treacherous brother and all the rest of it, and he has gone to the pools to see if his wife has returned.

Not his wife, in fact. If she returns she will just be a woman named Kaleithi whose face he will know, but who will not be bound to him. That much, Angilly understands. They take weddings seriously in Usmai, and not prince or pauper can just walk away without incurring the wrath of various divinities, from the invisible death-god of the old empire to the local frog deity. She's seen the frog god by now. Been admitted into its cave by its order of refreshingly non-stabby monks. It's a big frog. It's not all that. It was asleep. As gods go, she's seen better. Being a Pal, she's seen more impressive gods rendered down for their magic.

Here they all are, then, at the still, diamond-watered pools outside the lazing god's cave. Standing before that arch with its carvings of water weed and swimmers and eels. The Alkhand, standing like the lightning rod for all the world's melancholy. His court, the nobles and ministers and priests. His children, all of them this time. Gorbudan the Warrior, mighty hunter, the thought of whose accession to the throne keeps neighbouring rulers up at night. Dekamran, the educated, the quiet man who knows he won't ever amount to anything and so doesn't care about picking up a woman's sword to duel the Palleseen Resident now and then, or spending an evening drinking with her and trading school stories. The other two, the skinny youth with the unhealthy eyes and the sullen girl everyone mostly forgets about because she defiantly won't do the court princess bit. And then the others. Tarcomir, Angilly, a handful of observers from the neighbouring states, a Maric merchant who has no idea what's going on but whom the locals mistakenly thought was some manner of ambassador.

And the others. The lesser audience, who are waiting like the Alkhand, but are forced by his august presence to wait off to one side, supporting characters in their own play.

Three years before, the Alkhani Kaleithi walked into the pools. She entered the ranks of a monastic order, to serve under their rules for a couple of years in order to wash away the bonds of her life, that she might be free. Angilly feels this should stand as a repudiation of the Alkhand, that his wife wanted to leave him. Dekamran claims not, that this is just how things are in Usmai. She reckons that's the formal line, sure enough, but that human nature trumps custom sometimes.

And Kaleithi did nothing by halves. The city of Alkhalend has monks like a beggar has lice. There are even Louse Monks, in fact. If some artisan or labourer wants to sever their match to a spouse they can pick from a range of static or mendicant lives, spend their years doing good works or sweeping a garden or travelling from village to village telling stories and making tea. For those who feel the bonds of matrimony the strongest, though, stronger waters are required to dissolve them. For them there are the Alborandi, the monks of last resort. The mask-wearers.

Angilly doesn't understand the Alborandi. She's asked both Tarcomir and Dekamran, and come to the conclusion that, speculate as they might, neither do they. Donning that faceless mask is more than simply wearing a robe and handing out charity to the poor. Their duty is to maintain a certain sacred grove near the city. A site of historical and magical interest intricately interwoven with the history of Usmai. Far more than any other order, to join the Alborandi is to leave everything of your life behind.

One year ago, the Alkhand stood here at the pools on the first clear day after Thunder Month. The Alborandi came, a winding procession down from the cliffs above, walking all the way from their sacred grove. The masked priests stood in the water, just as they're doing now. Faceless, enigmatic. Angilly had felt a tension in the air and known it to be Mystery. That numinous baggage that certain gods and traditions bring with them, that strikes awe from the souls of men and women like sparks from flint. The thing the Pals are dedicated to obliterating from the world, because to be perfect means to be fully known and understood, hence mystery by its very nature is imperfection.

She sees the moment when it happens. Two or three of the monks abruptly standing differently. Lifting their hands to remove the timeworn wood of their masks and hand them away. Blinking as though they'd not seen the sun for a long time, and not just because of the rains. And some had walked to greet those who were waiting for them, and others just walked away. Each one free of whatever bonds they had sought to sever, permitted to start any new life they chose and could sustain, with no-one able to claim a hold over them. But none of them had been Kaleithi.

Something went out of the Alkhand on that day. Even though the woman who hadn't returned would not in any event have been his wife. Would have been able to just turn her back on him, the most powerful man in all Usmai, and depart. He would, Dekamran said, have been happy with that. To watch her back as she walked away from him. For at least then he would have a closed door in his life, and not one left eternally ajar. But she had not returned. The Alborandi had kept her, or she had loved the life that much, or some other thing covered by the shroud of their Mystery. The Alkhand had spent the next season barely holding court, barely eating, some said. Gorbudan and a variety of priests and ministers had tugged the nation one way and another. Dekamran had wept. When he was alone with Angilly. When he could permit himself the liberty. Wept because his mother was gone and he hadn't seen her go and now he hadn't seen her return.

And here they are, another year on, and the Alborandi stand in the pool with their robes soaking up the diamond water. The Mystery coils about them like an invisible snake and four of the masked figures shiver, and remove their masks. A balding old man, a girl of surely no more than twenty, a stout old matron, a cadaverous, dour man whose face is refinding its customary lines of disdain. Four very different people who, a moment ago, Angilly couldn't have told from one another. None of them the former Alkhani of Usmai.

She studies the Alkhand's face. He is outwardly stoic. His

stone eyes stare. Blind, but the very current of the crowd will have told him everything he needs to know. He is the ruler, though; the supreme power of Usmai. Life and death are in his mouth. He was a warrior prince too. Even blind, he defeated his brother in battle and in the hearts of the people, and look who's holding whose skull now. He is a scholar of verse and scripture who has the wisest and the most eloquent read to him each night, so that he too might increase his wisdom and eloquence. He has four living children, each one a cornucopia of gifts and qualities, even if only one of their names is on the lips of the people. His Tranquillity Alkhand Oparan of Usmai, no man for crass spectacle, a paragon of public poise.

He turns. The court hurriedly arranges itself in order of prominence so that they might process behind him properly. Angilly and Tarcomir find their places towards the back, the dignitaries just dignified enough to have a place there.

The Alkhand takes three steps away from the pools, the strong and confident stride of a blind man who still knows the way. He stops.

The court, just getting into its stride behind him, concertinas into chaos. Gorbudan, at the Alkhand's back, has of course halted at a perfect distance, but a senior monk barrels into him and retreats, ashen and apologising. The Alkhand Oparan turns his face to the cloudless skies he will never see and lets out a sound.

It is the sound of what was in Angilly's heart when her parents burned, or when she realised Benallers wasn't coming back. It is the grief that knows nothing of station, but comes to orphaned Pal children and foreign kings equally. She actually feels tears start in her eyes from it; unprofessional, imperfect, ridiculous. She glances at Tarcomir. His face is very set. And who doesn't have a tragedy in their life, a grief, a loss? Only those so blessed can be unmoved at the Alkhand's cry.

He tears his ornate, gold-threaded robe from his shoulders. Digs his fingers into his vest of gems and gold chains and enamelled plates, and rips it open. Loose jewels spill at his feet or dance into the glittering water of the pools. The Alkhand drops to his knees, beats his hands on the slick stone. His bare skin shows old scars, a map of all he won back in the day, and nothing that hurt him as much as the open door his wife left behind her.

At first Angilly thinks this is just some Usmiat custom she hasn't seen before, a public declaration of grief. But everyone's horribly embarrassed. The royal children exchange glances. This is *Not Done*. The Alkhand is not referred to as His Tranquillity for nothing. What is also Not Done is intruding onto that maelstrom of grief, offering aid, helping an old man to his feet as he weeps stone tears.

Dekamran is the one who breaks, of course. The soft one. The one exposed to foreign ways. Just one more reason he won't ever be challenging Gorbudan for the throne. He kneels by his father. He speaks soft words. He dares to take the Alkhand's elbow. He collects his father's shawl and settles it about the old man's shoulders. By this means the procession is permitted to start again, and can reach the palace where the Alkhand can retreat to his chambers, with his poets and his theologians, out of the eyes of local and foreign gawpers alike.

She and Tarcomir compare notes, later. They both agree this is a spectacularly bad time for the Alkhand of Usmai to start acting up. Because sufficient time and drink have now passed, between them and that dreadful cry, they can wear their dispassionate diplomat hats and discuss the foreigners as though they're slightly different and slightly less than civilized people. It's a show they put on for one another.

They're both getting the same dispatches from their respective homes. She from Outreach on the Archipelago, he from the Palatine Minister of Foreign Affairs in Lor. The two great powers of the world, as far as either is concerned. The nations whose influence has spread everywhere there's money to be made or influence to be claimed, on either side of the ocean. And the Pals have a habit of following up with armies where the Loruthi just want to own everything, but that still makes them the only two players on a board where everyone else is just a game piece.

"It will not, of course, come to anything," is Tarcomir's opinion. There are just the two of them at a screened-away table, their aides keeping their distance by mutual consent. Because this is one of the better hostelries with a veranda overlooking the waterfalls, there are channels of flowing water incised into the floor that bring a cool clarity to the air inside. The servants light scented candles floating in rose-glass bowls and serve sharp ramaht in little painted cups, then retreat to give the foreigners their privacy.

"Of course," Angilly agrees. They smile at one another, and for once it's not the usual diplomatic mendacity. The dispatches from their respective homes are increasingly hysterical regarding What Must Be Done about the other global power. Palleseen and Loruthi interests are clashing everywhere. All yesterday's amicable arrangements about leaving the other alone have gone to tatters very quickly. There have been skirmishes mercantile, political and now military. Certain quarters of the world are holding their breath.

"But if it does," says Tarcomir. Speaking not the Usmiri they're both quite fluent in now, but Pel, because even the Loruthi conduct most of their international business in the Pals' efficient, utilitarian language. "Should it," he says, hunting the words, "it will not come here. It need not. Between you and I."

"Of course," she repeats, and drinks. The ramaht is very sharp, biting the roof of her mouth. That's how you know it's the good stuff.

"Gorbudan crowned will be a calmer man than Gorbudan prince," Tarcomir says. "The robes of state will weigh him down. There will be concessions." He smiles at her. "Between you and me, this city could do with fewer monks and priests and the like. You want to pick an order to persecute, I'll make sure the word gets to the right ear. That will play well to Outreach, I think?"

It isn't patronising. It would indeed play well. She isn't going to go head to head with the somnolent frog god, but if she can tell her superiors she's encouraging the Usmiat to divest themselves of their irrational spirituality, one sect at a time, that will earn her another turn of the glass before she's replaced. Tarcomir, her enemy, values having a known quantity across the table from him. He'll do her some favours when the ear he's whispering in has the White Petal Crown balanced over it. That should be what she's worrying about, but it isn't.

It's the skull, really. That inlaid piece of regalia that the Alkhand carries about. Which contains, allegedly, the bound ghost of that very brother he had such a protracted struggle with to claim the throne. It's the skull, and it's the stone eyes of the Alkhand, a souvenir of the time his brother was winning that struggle. These things speak to the way things are done in the Successor States, when there is one throne and multiple children. And the daughter will get married off somewhere, Peor or Goshumai or Lucibi or somewhere further afield. And perhaps the youngest son is too skinny and callow and just straight-up weird to be a problem, but Dekamran is handsome and educated and, because of his soft nature, well-liked by many. Not least by her. And Gorbudan is the warrior prince, the sword-brandisher, the great hunter, leaping here and there about the country, doing heroic things. Not being soft, not even slightly.

What should concern her about Gorbudan's accession is that he favours the Loruthi over her own people. As Usmai carries the weight in this part of the world, that will shift the balance of power against the Pals dramatically. Her career will take a knock; she might be recalled. Nobody back home will be happy, and fair enough because she will have failed at her one job. But what concerns her is that probably Gorbudan will want a skull to play with too, and she knows just where he'll get it.

Four days later, word comes on the swiftest courier skiff out of Peor. War has been declared between Lor and Pallesand.

Behind the Mask

Not so long ago, she'd received word from Palinet, the Resident in Peor, via official courier on official boats flying official Palleseen flags. Theoretically that should still be the case, diplomatic protections working as they do. After a variety of interceptions and interruptions caused by the current uptick in coastal piracy, messengers turn up incognito, often not even Palleseen at all. And it's amazing how they don't seem to attract piratical attention the way a Pal uniform does.

The man who she lets in through the side door of Slate House, the Resident's residence, is a skinny Peost dressed up as a skinny Usmiat. She peruses his credentials while he shifts from foot to foot, then pours him a cup of blunt ramaht for his thirst. She's doing all these things because, on the general basis that inconvenient things love company, Storry is sick with one of the things foreigners get sick with on the Successor Coast. And he's lived here longer than her, and she'd have thought he'd developed resistances, but apparently there are still things that can either get you, or recur from some long-past infection. He's up in his room inhaling medicines she bought from the new foreign-run hospital off in the Sand Lanes, because they're supposed to be good, and the local remedies weren't helping. Storry will be on a boat back to the Archipelago if his health improves enough to make the trip, leaving her unsupported in the middle of a war.

A quiet war, in this part of the world. No clash of Loruthi and Palleseen armies and the Alkhand has stated and restated Usmai's neutrality. Except here's Palinet's messenger with a report, in encrypted Pel, of three more raids across the Usmiat–Peost border, Palleseen factoras, mills and plantations their main targets. Nothing catastrophic. No large-scale massacres, just a little looting and arson. The Peosts have suffered too, but it's mostly their foreign guests. And the Pals have their own soldiers who've been chasing up and down the border getting their uniforms soaked with sweat. But the raiders are swift, in and out and knowing the country, and the lumbering Palleseen war machine, such as it is in Peor, hasn't been able to catch them. Because they are disciplined and well-led.

Angilly nods over the report, grinding her teeth. She knows exactly who is leading the raiders. Everyone does, an open secret. When the business started she even tried to raise it at court, before the Alkhand. But the Alkhand is sunk in melancholy and hears only poets and scholars and musicians, and then only sad ones. And the other functionaries of the court know exactly whose favour they need to secure, and so deny everything to her face. There are no raids. Or it is brigands. Probably those Peosts fighting one another. Or Peosts attacking Pals, you know how they are. And who, in Usmai, would care about any of that?

Gorbudan, when he is at court, nods along with a slight smile, and makes some sly remark to Tarcomir, the Loruthi emissary. When he is not at court he sallies from his fortress at Mantekor and leads his raiders across the Peost border to pillage Palleseen holdings. Everyone knows and nobody says and increasingly Angilly looks the weak fool.

And there's damn all she can do about it, and she writes a polite note to Palinet to that general effect. She has never got anywhere near Gorbudan, and the man's charisma means there's no way of suborning some discontented follower for intel, because they're all quite content, thank you. All of them happy to charge about in the wake of their warrior prince leader who's going to be Alkhand sooner rather than later. And then let both Pals and Peosts watch out because Usmai is long overdue some muscle-flexing.

There is a whole room of traders and travellers, Pals all, who want a bite of her time. They've been insulted, they've been robbed, they've been taxed, they've had their livelihoods confiscated. Not unreasonably, they want to know what *their* Resident is going to do about it. And her answer to them would be some variation on her reply to Palinet and so she dodges out through the same side door and seeks other company. She's prepared a very specific document, that frankly pushes the furthest boundary of her authority but she reckons she'd be able to argue the case back home. When she's in the top room of a prestigious hostelry near the waterfalls, she presses it into the hand of Dekamran, the second son.

He reads it. It's in Pel but so was his education, so it's no barrier. His eyebrows go way up that high familial forehead. The one that looks fierce on Gorbudan but just mildly surprised on him.

"Really?" he asks her. "Gil?"

"Really," she says. Four years of acquaintance have

ironed out the *Sier*s from her address. Sometimes *Fammi*, the equivalent of 'mate' to a Pal, of familiar equals, but she doesn't feel that informal right now. She is acting in her official capacity.

"The Archipelago," he says. "I suppose I always did want to see it."

"There's a ship due in dock this month," she says, knowing that the pirates are bold and don't just stick to the coast any more, but what can she do? "Storry's going home. There's a berth for you. The master's own, if I ask it."

"I hate to say it, Gil," Dekamran has that awkward smile about him, half laughing at himself, half at everything else risible in the world, "but if I was to be the Usmiat ambassador to the Archipelago, wouldn't my father need some say in that? Unless it's different where you come from. Have you been fooling us all this time? You were never formally appointed this, you just turned up one day and decided, *I know, I'll be the Resident for a bit?* Only I didn't think that was how it works."

"There's always a surprising amount of finagle, in diplomacy," she tells him. "Once you're there, in place, it will make more sense for the court to accept the status quo than challenge it."

"Post facto diplomacy," he says. "Remarkable idea. I know what this is about, Gil."

A chill, sad feeling passes over her, despite the heat. "Well of course you do. If you were dumb enough not to, I wouldn't trust you with the ambassadorship."

"You don't think much of my brother."

"I think he's currently setting fire to my countryfolk across the border, with the tacit backing of the Loruthi," she said flatly. "I think that, when the war's over and we've won, Usmai will be very glad of an ambassador on the Archipelago."

"You don't think very much of me."

She felt a peculiar pain in her, an open wound she thought had been sewed shut a long time ago. After Benallers. "Well I am one of those arrogant *Kepishi* and you're all ignorant superstitious foreigners. Obviously."

"You don't think I can protect myself."

She thinks of the skull. "This is a valuable diplomatic—"

"I can't go. My father needs me here. Gorbudan doesn't spend much time at his bedside, what with – all right, what with all the raiding he's doing strictly against my father's dictates. Fine. He needs me, Gil. He needs me just *here*, in the palace, in the city. Because my younger brother does nothing but learn mantras and play with bones and my sister – well, you know how she is."

The youngest scion of the Alkhand has become quite the wild one. Seen in all the wrong parts of the city, associating with the wrong people. She challenged Angilly at skiamachy a week before, and while the kid's still a way off being *good*, she's become a lot better now she has some foreign maverick to teach her all the dirty street-fighting tricks. Because, Angilly suspects, she has a much clearer idea of what Gorbudan's accession will mean than Dekamran does. Or that he will admit, anyway.

She does not beg. Her professional dignity will not allow it. She makes the pleasant talk with Dekamran, that weird communion that exists outside the tightening laces of her formal role. It's only him and Tarcomir she can unwind with, honestly. Her friend and her enemy. She does not beg. That would be inappropriate to her professional dignity. She does not plead with him to take the letter and the ship, though it's in every gesture and tilt of her head.

That done – that task failed, like so many of her tasks – she does not return to the Residency and all those offended Pals who want to bitch at her. She loses herself in the city, instead. Absolutely against regulations, but with Storry laid up, nobody's around to keep her straight. And she's slowly given over various pieces of the uniform, traded them in for the local dress that is so much better suited to the climate. The dampened robe over her shoulders, a short vest cinched at the side, the Pal-pattern buttons sewn into its bodice just a nod to militaristic dress. Baggy thin trousers cinched at the ankle and petal-cuffed soft boots. And her sword, the one wrong note. The Pal rapier she prefers to a local skia because she's more used to the balance.

She spends some time in the Sand Lanes, listening to the poorest of the locals talk politics with a knowledge that would impress a spymaster. She passes by the hospice, the Fever Lodge they're calling it, where they have a fresh batch of Storry's medicines. She goes to the docks and hears what the sailors are saying about pirates and where their pirated plunder actually ends up. It's better than having a network of informants at her beck and call.

She goes to the pools and sits there in quiet contemplation, letting the spray cool her and soak into her shawl. She has a terrible sense of a great many things coming to an end.

The Palleseen Resident in Alkhalend does not, of course, just jaunt off on foot across the city, unaccompanied. Anything could happen. One of the other things she does not under any circumstance do, one of the things that does, in fact, happen, is just leaving. Not even on a boat. Finding an official who owes her a favour, securing passage north into the jungles. Past the pleasure houses of the rich that line the top of the cliffs to peer down at the House of Tranquillity and the Constellar Gardens. Past the estates and farms and into the jungle.

The thing she rides on, as one last-minute added passenger, is inextricably tied up with the place she is going to and the history of Usmai. After the old moribund empire fell – *Moeribandi*, in fact, the name of the empire giving rise to the Pel word – its various parts immediately set to fighting one another. The reason Usmai became the dominant force this side of the mountains, and not Peor or Lucibi, say, was that it had more and stranger resources to draw upon.

This beast is vast, the size of a small house at least. Its hide is scaled. A long barbed tail swings behind, and three savage curved horns ahead, set before a great shield of a head. She rides on a howdah along with a couple of Usmiat merchants or scholars, and a lizard. It is a lizard as long in the body as a human, with a sharp-snouted head and huge bright-coloured eyes, and it wears a vest like an Usmiat, and holds a goad with which it hooks at their beast when it shows signs of wanting to deviate from the path through the jungle. A path mostly made by beasts just like this, that are owned and goaded by lizards. Lizards that do a lot of people-things, up to and including having their own district outside Alkhalend where some kind of queen-lizard broods clutches of enormous eggs, but still lizards. They come from the Grove.

The Usmiat word for the Grove is very long and hard

to say, and eventually Angilly understood this was because it was not an Usmiat word, but an attempt at borrowing from some other language entirely. Not lizard-language. The language of the Grove's keepers, the Alborandi. The nearest approximation, in Pel, is the Waygrove, so that is how she thinks of it.

The Waygrove is just a particular stand of trees deep in the jungle, close to Alkhalend. It is also the gateway to other places. It is not the only such place, she's heard, but she's never been posted anywhere else that made such a claim. Over Usmai's history, a variety of groups have come out of the Waygrove, refugees or adventurers from grand elsewheres nobody ever heard of. Some of them were granted a home here, and in return they lent their talents to their new nation. The species of beast Angilly is currently swaying atop is the armoured, unstoppable fist of Usmai's armies, and the reason that nobody is getting in Gorbudan's way when he decides to cross the Peost border en masse. And there are other special servants of the throne, but they all come from the Waygrove. Historically, the only time Usmai's ambitions have been curtailed were when all the other states banded together or when the nation was divided against itself. Which happens a lot, but she doesn't think Gorbudan is going to let things go that way. Hence her offer to Dekamran.

Hence her being here on this *thing*, going to this *place*. Something no self-respecting and rational Pal would do without three squads of troopers and a writ from the Commission.

It's two days on beast-back from the top of the cliffs to the Waygrove, because the lumbering monsters stop for nothing. There is a compound there, where the Alborandi live. The mask-wearers. Those who give themselves into the service of the Grove, and sometimes return, and sometimes do not. Angilly climbs down the scaly side of the beast and realises she has no idea what comes next.

She stands there, and the masked monks come and go. Some are men, some women, tall, short, a few perhaps not even local. Perhaps even pale as a Pal can be after a few years of Usmiat sun, like her. Yet there is a strangeness and a sameness to them, and she finds herself incapable of knowing, after glancing away, which of a group of monks she has seen before, and which are new. And they come and collect supplies from the beast, and seem to engage in some communion with the lizard mahout, and tend gardens and place offerings in niches, and not a word is spoken between them. And none of them look at her even with their eyeless masks.

The sense of their Mystery is very strong, now. All around her. A place she should not have come to. As a Pal. As a human being.

Within their compound, right at the back, the palisade opens up and there are just trees. Jungle trees, such as clothe the land from here to the foothills, yet the gap in their wall makes them a gateway, and through the gateway are many places.

She speaks to them, introducing herself, titles and stations. She is come from the Palleseen Archipelago. Perhaps they've heard of it? She is from Alkhalend and she knows they've heard of *that*. She has papers. She is important. She has pressing business with… whoever is in charge.

Nobody is in charge. Nobody stands forward in a fancier robe and a more decorated mask. They do not consent to knowledge of the Archipelago or Alkhalend. They do not consent to *her*.

She enters the compound. Which she knows is a thing

that she expressly is not permitted to do. Her hand on her sword, which she knows will not help. Waiting for them to explode into outraged action to expel her. Waiting for their foreign sorcery. But they do nothing. She feels that, if she looked behind her, she'd see no tracks in the earth from her boots. She doesn't exist here. Which means she can go where she will.

Ahead is the gap in the wall, the framed trees, the Waygrove. She could go anywhere. The thought is more terrifying to her than the fire. Like an abyss, limitless and hungry, at her very feet.

"Excuse me," she says, and "Please," in Usmiri and Pel, and a few other languages she's had cause to learn. Jarokiri, Faraslendi, Allorwen. Her words go through them like ghosts. She reaches out, steels herself, tugs at sleeves. They are whisked from between her fingers. She stands in their way and they walk around her without seeing her. Or, she feels, she is just shifted sideways by the world and they don't divert their course at all.

Night falls eventually, after an hour or so of this pantomime. Here in the jungle it comes swiftly, as the canopy swallows the sun. She's left out in the start of what feels like misting rain that will last until dawn. Sage-Invigilator Angilly, thirty-seven years old, Palleseen Resident in Usmai, reaches her limit. In a quiet, diplomatic way. Crouches down by the curve of the palisade wall near that gap she absolutely will not cross. Back to the stakes, sitting on her haunches, her hands like claws as she drags at her hair in frustration, ripping it from its regulation Pal bun until it straggles down her shoulders. Eyes wide, teeth bared, a beast in a trap. Weeping behind the cage of those teeth. Because she couldn't save her parents and she couldn't save Benallers and now she won't be able to save Dekamran. The fact that her career and her posting here and the local influence of the Palleseen Sway are also on the executioner's block doesn't even come into it. She just wants to do this one thing, accomplish this one good thing.

It wasn't true when she started the journey. It won't be true when she returns to Alkhalend, but in this moment she discovers that, no, it *is* true. That one unprofessional thing is what she wants, and she can't have it.

One of the Alborandi, the monks of the Grove, crouches down next to her. For a moment her heart leaps, but behind the mask is a heavyset man's frame, swag-bellied and heavy, a knife-fighter's scars across bare forearms. He's not being companionable, either. His pose mimics hers, even down to gripping the edge of his mask where she rakes her hair. He's mocking her in mime.

She waits for him to go. He doesn't. He's not who she's here to try and talk to. He's not a leader. He's most certainly not Kaleithi, wife of the Alkhand. Yet, in the end, she tells him. Because she's here and the words are inside her, and they're a weight of goods she doesn't want to haul undelivered all the way back to Alkhalend.

She tells his mask about the lost wife and mother, and that becomes telling it about the old blind man who doesn't know what his life is for now she's gone, and that becomes telling it about Dekamran. She is not diplomatic. She draws an outline made of all his flaws. Too weak, too sensitive, too mild, too foolish. And somehow the shape within that line is something virtuous. Someone, a living human being, whom she has grown to like. Not because he was educated by people like her, and not because he might be a useful tool for people like her, and certainly not because he has that ephemeral royal blood business, but just for himself. The words come out of her, inappropriate, disordered, not a one of them with a stamp of approval from the Commission of Ends and Means. And then they're done and that's all of them, and she's like a bag emptied out onto the ground. Staring down at what has come out of her and wondering at how little of value there really was.

"Anyway," she puts into the resultant silence. "That was it. That was me. I'll go back tomorrow. I'll sleep on the beast, in the howdah. If the lizard'll let me." And then, because the silence is still there and hungry, "How about you?"

The mask tilts to look at her. It does not tell her how about itself, or anything. The Alborandi monk stands, as though not entirely sure why it was down there in the first place, and remembering that it had important inscrutable monk business elsewhere.

The lizard will indeed let her sleep on the howdah. Or at least she asks it in her decent Usmiri and its nodding and hissing seem to indicate consent. The beast itself has gone down on its belly and knees, chomping desultorily at a great manger of leaves and stems. Its innards rumble like distant thunder, but that somehow brings on sleep, rather than staving it away. The sun wakes her, and she has a chance to stretch her legs and wash before the animal is goaded onto its feet and made ready for the return journey. She wonders if she should feel cleansed of some burden perhaps. She doesn't. Or she feels that she, the rational Pal, should be disgusted at herself for seeking solace in this heathen superstition, but she doesn't feel that either. She doesn't really feel much of anything. It's time for her to go back and watch Tarcomir do well for himself and hope that, when he's swanning around with a staff of Loruthi advisors at the new Alkhand's court, he'll throw her a bone or two so he can keep her around.

When she goes to climb up into the howdah again, one of the Alborandi stands in her way. The intrusion is so unexpected she actually treads on a bare foot before she can stop. The masked monk makes no complaint, nor even flinches. It isn't the same one as last night. Shorter, stockier, a woman maybe.

"Excuse me," Angilly says. She could just step to one side. There's no reason whatsoever she shouldn't just detour around this unusually obstructive monk. She doesn't, and doesn't know why.

The mask has no eyeholes, just dashes of paint without pattern. She saw the monks retouching the masks just yesterday. Finger-dabbling the colours onto the old wood with the singular focus of children. Painstakingly recreating designs that have no logic or meaning to them. And which, though all different, all look the same.

The monk thrusts an arm out to her, something swinging and jangling from the hand. Angilly takes it by instinct and the monk is gone. Walks away without any admission that they had stopped. Lost moments later amongst other monks, impossible to pick out from even a handful of their fellows.

Angilly's throat is very dry. She looks at what she has been given.

She knows what it is. She does not know what it might accomplish. Maybe everything. Maybe nothing. Maybe only terrible, bad things. Not odds she'd want to stake her career on, surely.

She climbs up into the howdah.

★

Back at Alkhalend she spends the morning listening to and dismissing the various plaintiffs thronging the waiting room at Slate House. Tells each in no uncertain terms there's nothing she can do, while in the lion's share of her mind she wonders whether she's going to do *it*.

After lunch, after checking on Storry and going through the sparse correspondence her aide isn't able to field for her any more, she puts pen to paper. Her handwriting, that is functional as a Pal's should be, but not elegant like Storry's. Dark Pal ink. Thick Loruthi paper, ironically enough, because they make the best. And the message itself will be meagre so she should at least make up for that with good materials.

She writes a brief and anonymous note, as from an unknown friend, explaining just who is responsible for this piece of memory finding its way back to the right hands, then anoints the paper with her personal seal and the Resident's stamp in red ink, so there can be no confusion over just which anonymous party is behind this incredibly foolish thing.

Into a pouch she places the note and what the monk gave her. In the palace she finds the servants and functionaries who owe her the most and burns her entire store of hoarded favours so that she might be brought in private to the Alkhand. To hear, so the pretence goes, his favourite poet perform. The reading is beautiful and she is wound too tense to appreciate it. Instead, at the end she stands and begs for permission to present a gift. Places the pouch in the hands of the poet who places it into the hands of the Alkhand.

The poet reads the note aloud in his clear, elegant voice. Only he and the old man and she share the secret, and Usmiat poets are professional confidantes among other things.

She returns to the Residence and waits, thinking, *I could have bought a house on the Archipelago.* Maybe that was the true meaning, and she'd missed it. That she could have cut and run, gone home. Sold the absurdly ornamented thing and retired to obscurity. A necklace of gold and amber in the spiralling shape of a tree could buy off a lot of failure, even from Correct Speech.

But word would still have reached her, from Usmai. There's nowhere in the world she could go, where it wouldn't track her down. So, instead, this.

Three days later she's at court again. Not for any better reason than that's where she, the Resident, is expected to be. Court is almost an afterthought to the nation now. A place for the Alkhand to sit and be melancholy in view of a crowd, rather than just the select company of some musician and a poet in his chambers. Nobody's expecting much of it. Certainly nobody is expecting what happens.

Some functionary is reciting a long, tedious list of trivial matters, judicial decisions perhaps or maybe provincial appointments. In all honesty Angilly has tuned it out. She only registers when the woman's rather grating voice chokes to sudden silence.

The Alkhand has stood.

"Bring me," he says, "my son."

He has three sons but nobody puzzles over which one he means. Gorbudan is in the palace, as it happens, though by tomorrow he'll be off for Mantekor and that band of lusty border raiders nobody's admitting he keeps. He is fetched, and performs the appropriate obeisance to his father the Alkhand. Of all the people there, he is expecting what comes next least of all.

The Alkhand's voice is a weak reed these days, everyone knows. He is consumed by a noble sorrow. The eyes that see nothing have communicated their blindness to his mind. His country governs itself in his name, with his nod, without his active involvement. No longer does he stand in court and make decrees without a thousand functionaries filtering his utterance for meaning and, if they find none, inserting their own. Command was the way of the old days, while he battled his brother, while he had the support of his wife. Not the way of this old husk of a thing, the cocoon that his son's energetic rule must soon hatch out of.

"You have broken my decree," the Alkhand tells his eldest son. "You have taken your followers into Peor. You have set upon the *Kepishi* of Pallesand, at the behest of the envoy of their enemy." The air in court is so still Angilly's amazed anyone can draw it into their lungs. "In this clash of foreign powers, in which I have decreed Usmai stands neutral, you have taken a side, and made me a *liar*." And the old man's mad; fire-furious and yet utterly controlled. A monarch, a leader of men, the man who took the head of the brother who blinded him. And Angilly actually hears it, the echo of a voice from that ornamented skull sitting on the arm of the throne. "*Liar*," spits the dead brother's ghost in disgust at the disobedience of his nephew.

Gorbudan's eyes are wide, but everyone there save his father sees that the first place he looks is to Tarcomir, the Loruthi. The accusation pierces all dissimulation and the incriminating bond between the two is as plain as if there was a rope binding them together.

"Father." Gorbudan, the leader of men, the warrior prince, stammers. "You do not understand. These Palleseen, they are killers of gods, devourers of ways. We must drive them from us, or they will make us their slaves, as they have the Peosts."

"You have made me a *liar*," spits the Alkhand, the iron rage still on him. "You have buried me before my time. You have told the world that the White Petal Crown sits on your brow, and that this throne is yours. You have placed your words in my mouth." And everyone has known these things for months, for a year, and nobody said anything, least of all the Alkhand.

"You have your saddlebags packed to go to Mantekor, I know," says the Alkhand. "Go, then. But take with me my curse. Any who ride with you against the Palleseen are banished from my court. Their ghosts shall know no quiet here. I shall have the Moerends harry them into the sea where they shall know no peace for a thousand years."

Easy for a rational Pal to scoff at such superstition, save that the priesthood inherited from the Dead Empire is rife with necromancers and the doom the old man threatens is a very real one. Angilly shivers and she's not the only one.

Gorbudan nods. He's been banished before. He knows how it goes. His father will cool. He will be back.

"Bring me my son," says the Alkhand.

Gorbudan, who had been backing away in the approved manner, pauses in confusion. A wrinkle on that warlike brow. And for a moment the functionaries dither and everyone looks sidelong at each other and nobody is quite sure what is going on. In the end she herself must jab Dekamran in the ribs so that he understands and steps forward.

"Of all my children it is you, the dutiful," the Alkhand says, blind yet his hand finds his second son's soft shoulder sure enough. "You, the obedient. You, my heir."

She tells nobody, and nobody tells. Tarcomir and Gorbudan certainly try and find out just how it all fell apart just as they were at the very apex of their swing, so that when the blade came down, it was their plan with its head in the basket and not the Pals'. But Gorbudan is banished to Mantekor, and Tarcomir is suddenly not the man that people want to speak to, or do favours for, and so neither ever discover about the letter or what was in the bag.

Dekamran tries to find out, too, but while he is certainly now the man people want to speak to, he is perhaps not hard enough to ask the hard questions. He never knows just what it was that bribed his father into valuing and elevating him.

What Angilly never knows is just what the Alkhand does with the necklace, after. A king's ransom of exquisite jewellery, enough to buy that modest house on the Archipelago that she'll probably never afford now. The unique piece that Kaleithi wore, when she stepped into the pools, and that the Alkhand probably gave her, perhaps even on the day they were wed. And it wasn't what she'd gone to the Waygrove to bring back. She'd wanted to bring back the *woman*, his wife, Dekamran's mother, and Gorbudan's. Perhaps just so she'd sort out the increasingly venomous knot within the family. But there was no woman to bring back. Just a lot of mask-wearing monks. Or, as she sometimes wonders, monk-wearing masks. And, behind them, nobody. And perhaps, for some, being nobody is easier, and they don't ever want to go back to having a face and a family and other painful, complicated things. And perhaps – probably even – she doesn't understand the Alborandi, what they are and what they do. But they understood her well enough to give her a message to pass on. Not the return of a wife, but at least the certain knowledge that the wife will not return. A closing of a door that was only letting in a leaching chill from unhealthy places. Little enough, you'd think, for the Alkhand to be grateful for. And yet, delivered in Dekamran's name, and under her seal, it had been enough. Because it hadn't been Kaleithi gone that had been eating the old man alive, it had been the not knowing. And now he knows.

The next report she sends home – with Storry the invalid – is a sight more positive than she's been able to write for years. The next that Tarcomir sends back will be rather more difficult to draft. Certainly, when she puts out overtures, there is nothing left of that easy camaraderie they had, two foreigners together. That's just one of the things she's burned.

And the war moves towards its conclusion, through turns and reversals and escalation, wedging itself between them so that what might have been bridged becomes a chasm that could swallow armies. A year later, in the very shadow of the war's end, their own personal war ends too, Tarcomir's blood on her blade. He's dead, she's alive, Pallesand in the ascendant and Dekamran set to inherit, and it doesn't feel like winning.

Author's Note

I am noted as a somewhat prolific author, so the genesis of this book is perhaps the most on-brand thing I've ever accomplished. When I'd done the preliminary work for *Days of Shattered Faith*, it became clear that – unlike its predecessors – the book would be focusing far more on one main character, Angilly. Who, then, was Angilly? The world of the Tyrant Philosophers is a complex and many-faceted one, and Angilly, as a product of its influences, was somebody I felt I needed to understand in detail before following her about the streets of Alkhalend. I would, therefore, exercise myself by writing a few brief vignettes detailing some formative events in her early life. You know, just a thousand words or so.

It turns out that Sage-Invigilator Angilly of Slate House had a lot of formative events in her life, which themselves filled out a great deal of supporting detail about how her world functioned. In the succession of little stories I wrote about her, I discovered how the Pals do espionage, the evolving history of conjuration in the Schools, Tallifer and Lochiver's resistance years in Jarokir, the pre-war situation in Bracinta, and of course Angilly's start in Usmai and just what she did to swing the political situation there back into line with Pal – and her own – desires. In short, my little writing exercise accidentally became an entire novella that served to expand the frontiers of the setting considerably.

As with everything else in this series (to date; we'll see if I can keep this particular tightrope walk up!), *Lives of Bitter Rain* can be read on its own, before or after *Days of Shattered Faith*. Read before, the start of *Faith* should hit differently, given the additional context. Rather than coming to Alkhalend as clueless as Loret, the reader is as wise as Angilly herself to the ways of Usmai, and of Palleseen skulduggery. Read after, the knowledge of what will come to pass should add a certain depth to the actions she takes in Usmai, and to the friendship with Tarcomir that you know to be as doomed as Benallers' maternal homeland. The series, after all, is about small people being caught in the wheels of history. Sometimes a foreknowledge of the path of those wheels adds to the emotional depth of the narrative.

While I have the pulpit, I also want to say how much fun this series, and world, is to write. As I've noted in more than one interview, this is the series I don't plan out. I build the world and then wander the streets of these cities, the wild places, the battlefields, holding my notebook and recording what I find there. Chronicling the actions of my cast as they struggle against, evade or fall before the great events they – even Angilly, even the Alkhand – have so little influence over. I plan a few more outings in the series before turning my yen for the fantastic elsewhere, but I feel this is a setting I'll always want to return to, and I hope you're enjoying it even half as much as I am.